THE 6TH GRADE NICKNAME GAME

Also by Gordon Korman

Born to Rock

Jake, Reinvented

The Juvie Three

Maxx Comedy

No More Dead Dogs

Schooled

Son of the Mob

Son of the Mob: Hollywood Hustle

THE 6TH GRADE NICKNAME GAME

gordon korman

Disney • HYPERION
Los Angeles New York

First Hardcover Edition, March 1999
First Paperback Edition, June 2000
Second Paperback Edition, September 2004
New Paperback Edition, June 2017

10 9 8 7 6 5 4 3 2 1
FAC-025438-17076
Printed in the United States of America

This book is set in 12-point Janson Text LT Pro/Fontspring

Library of Congress Control Number for Hardcover Edition: 98012343
ISBN 978-1-4847-9840-9
Visit www.DisneyBooks.com

To the schools I've visited;
thanks for the nicknames

THE NICKNAMERS

THE SUBSTITUTE TEACHER must have been six-feet-five, and solid as an oak tree. He shrugged his massive shoulders out of his warm-up jacket, revealing a barrel chest and giant muscles rippling under his T-shirt.

In the back row, Wiley Adamson opened his notebook to a clean page, and wrote: *King Kong?*

At the next desk, Jeff Greenbaum examined the paper critically. His brown eyes narrowed, as they always did when he was deep in thought. Deliberately, he reached out his pencil and drew a line through the nickname. Below it, he printed: *The Incredible Hulk?*

Wiley flashed a grudging grin of admiration, but

he crossed that one out too, and added: *Tiny?*

This brought a snicker from Jeff, which he swallowed when the new teacher began to speak.

"I guess I don't look very much like Mrs. Regan." He chuckled in a deep voice. This was true. The regular teacher stood four-feet-nine, and was wispy and white-haired. She had just retired to Florida. "I'll be taking over this class until a permanent replacement is found."

An uncomfortable murmur passed through the room. It wasn't so bad losing Mrs. Regan, and having a sub was usually a license to goof off. But this sub was obviously no pushover. He looked like the Terminator.

Through the speech, Wiley and Jeff continued to trade ideas.

Hercules?

Mr. E. Normous?

But nothing seemed just right. And if there was anything the two nicknamers of 6B knew for certain, it was that a true nickname had to fit perfectly.

"Now, some of you might recognize me as the assistant coach of the football team over at the high school," the big teacher was saying. "I never expected to wind up in sixth grade but, you know, with budget cuts—"

Musclehead?
Conan the Grammarian?

He picked up the chalk and wrote his name on the board. "I'm Mr. Hughes."

Wiley and Jeff exchanged a look of pure delight.

Peter Widman was the leadoff hitter in the softball game at recess. He already had a nickname, courtesy of Wiley and Jeff. Because of the thin blond streak in his jet-black hair, he was known affectionately as Skunk. He tapped his bat on home plate and assumed his stance.

"Hey, Skunk," said Wiley from his catcher's crouch. "What do you think of Mr. Huge?"

Peter stared at him for a moment, then threw back his head and laughed. "Mr. Huge!" he cackled. "I get it. That's funny!"

"What's the holdup?" called Jeff from the pitcher's mound.

"We're talking about Mr. Huge!" roared Peter.

Jeff pretended not to understand. "You mean Mr.

Hughes?" he yelled back with a wink aimed at Wiley.

"No, Mr. *Huge*!"

Peter got a hit. Soon he and the first baseman were laughing over the new nickname. When Peter stole second and then third, the entire infield was brought in on the joke. By the end of the inning, the word was out. Raymond Vaughn, the shortstop, had even taught himself how to burp "Mr. Huge" at top volume. Most of what Raymond said was communicated by a series of belches. This talent had earned him the nickname Gasbag.

"Mr. Huge" spread through the softball game like a case of measles. Every few seconds a burst of laughter or shout of approval sprang up as the new nickname was passed from mouth to mouth.

"Mr.—Oh, I get it! Because he's so big!"

"And his name—Hughes, Huge—"

"Why didn't *I* think of that?"

Wiley looked at his watch. "Eleven minutes and forty-five seconds."

"That's got to be our fastest time ever," Jeff said proudly.

Then the bush in front of them sneezed. Charles Rossi sprang up out of the scratchy branches.

"I'm onto you guys!" he raged. "Don't think I can't

see what you're up to. You just got everybody to call the new teacher Mr. Huge."

Wiley shrugged. "The guy's enormous and his name is Hughes. It was only a matter of time before somebody came up with it."

"But you did. You do it all the time," Charles accused them. "I'll bet it's like a game to you jerks."

Wiley snorted in disgust. "Ignore him," he advised Jeff. "You know what this is about, and it has nothing to do with Mr. Huge. Charles just doesn't like being called Snoopy."

Charles Rossi's face turned beet red. If looks could kill, Wiley and Jeff would have fallen down dead right on the spot. "Snoopy is a stupid nickname! A mean nickname! A *dog's* nickname!"

"Face it," Jeff said reasonably. "You know why everyone calls you Snoopy? Because you spend more time minding other people's business than your own."

Wiley nodded in agreement. "Where did we find you just now? In the bushes, snooping."

"I was not!" Charles raged. "I was tying my shoe. *You're* the ones who thought up Snoopy. And you blabbed it all over the world. Exactly like you just did with Mr. Huge!"

Jeff rolled his eyes. "If Snoopy was a bad nickname

nobody else would even bother repeating it. You're Snoopy because you're the biggest snoop in school. It's a well-known fact that a nickname will never stick if it's not the right one."

"Baloney!" Charles accused. "You can make any name stick if you say it often enough."

"No way," said Jeff.

"We'll prove it," Wiley added. "Pick a kid—any kid—and we'll give him a nickname that's totally, completely, absolutely wrong. You'll see. It won't stick."

Charles's eyes narrowed. "What's in it for me if *I'm* right?"

Wiley shrugged. "What have you got in mind?"

"I want a new nickname," Charles said instantly. "A good nickname. A *person's* nickname."

"It's a deal," agreed Jeff. With a sweep of his arm, he indicated the playground. "All we need now is a guinea pig for our experiment."

The three looked around. Most of the softball players already had nicknames. Kelly Warnover was known as Warmed-Over-Leftovers; Christy Jones was Crusty Bones; Gordon Wu's monster appetite had earned him the title Smorgas-Gord; identical twin brothers Dinky and Stan were dubbed Stinky and Dan; and of course, Gasbag and Skunk.

"I've got it," said Charles. "Him."

Wiley and Jeff followed the direction of his pointing finger. There stood Mike Smith, a tall blond boy from 6A. Mike was in the midst of a spirited game of dodgeball, but he definitely wasn't participating. He wasn't even watching. Actually, he wasn't doing anything.

Wiley and Jeff groaned in unison. They knew it wasn't going to be easy to come up with a nickname, good *or* bad, for Mike Smith. Mike was simply the blandest student in the history of Old Orchard Public School (called OOPS, thanks to the two nicknamers). He was neither happy nor unhappy. He didn't really have any friends, but no one was his enemy. What was he like? What was his favorite food? Did he watch TV? Was he a sports fan? Computer nerd? Musician? *Martian?* Nobody really knew.

"Come on, Snoopy," Wiley wheedled. "Pick somebody else. That guy's so *nothing!* If we can't figure out what he *is*, how can we nickname him what he *isn't?*"

Charles folded his arms in front of him. "He's my choice."

Jeff threw his hands in the air. "What are you supposed to call a blob like that—Iceman?"

"That's it!" crowed Wiley. "Iceman!" He turned to

Charles. "If that name sticks, I'll eat your backpack!"

The bell rang to signal the end of recess. Wiley, Jeff, and Charles joined the parade to the door.

Charles elbowed Jeff in the ribs. "I don't hear anything."

Jeff frowned. "What are you listening for—bird calls?"

Charles gestured toward Mike Smith. "You have to call him Iceman. You know, spread it around. Just like you did with Mr. Huge."

Jeff looked helpless. "I feel so stupid. He's about as cool as a loaf of bread. Why don't *you* do it, Snoopy?"

"It only works when it's you."

"Oh, all right," sighed Wiley. He waved at Mike and piped up, "Hey, Iceman!"

The tall boy from 6A didn't even look up. They were obviously talking to somebody else.

Wiley nudged Jeff. "This is one bet we can't lose."

BREAK!

MR. HUGHES TAUGHT sixth grade exactly the same way he coached high school football.

"Men—" He always referred to the class as men, even though twelve of the students were girls. "Men, this math quiz is *tough*. This may be the biggest challenge we've ever faced together as a team."

The class listened, stunned. The teacher was acting like this pop quiz was the Super Bowl. The papers were tucked in an iron grip in the crook of his arm as he stood before them, poised for flight like a halfback. His face reddened in concentration. A thin film of perspiration beaded his upper lip.

Wiley answered Jeff's unspoken question. "No, he's still Mr. Huge. But he's nuts."

"Maintain your intensity level," the teacher advised. "Stay focused on your opponents."

Christy Jones raised her hand. "Uh, sir? What opponents?"

Mr. Hughes stared at her in disbelief. "What opponents? Only long division, improper fractions, and the twelve times table! An all-star team of hazards and easy mistakes! But we've trained long and hard to get here," the teacher continued, placing a quiz facedown on each desk. "We're no pushovers! We can *fight!*"

Charles reached for his paper, and Mr. Hughes popped a whistle in his mouth and blew three sharp blasts. "False start!" He waited until all the students were poised motionless above their tests. The whistle blew. "*Break!*"

The class sat frozen. Finally, Peter raised his hand. "We get a break already?" he asked in confusion. "We haven't even started yet."

"No, no, no," said the big teacher. "Break! Like 'break the huddle.' In football, 'break' is the signal that talk is over; it's time for action."

"You mean 'start'?" ventured Gordon.

"I mean break!" exclaimed Mr. Hughes.

6B turned their attention to their papers. It was a routine quiz with only ten questions. Wiley and Jeff, who were both good at math, finished in the first five minutes. They spent the rest of the time watching Mr. Hughes, who was jogging between the rows of desks, barking out instructions like, "Come on, men! Let's give it a hundred-and-ten percent!" and "Keep your breathing steady!"

Actually, the only breathing problems were coming from the teacher himself. He was galloping around the room, gasping out encouragement. Sweat streamed down his face.

"He's like a real football player," whispered Jeff in awe.

"During a ninety-eight-yard punt return," added Wiley.

Mr. Hughes popped open a half-gallon bottle of Gatorade and downed it in three colossal gulps. He didn't seem to notice that most of 6B had already finished the easy quiz—and that *he* was the center of amazed attention.

"Two minute warning!" he cried.

Only Christy and Raymond were still working. They struggled to concentrate with the new teacher raving in their faces.

"Come on, Crusty!" piped up Wiley.

"Attaway, Gasbag!" added Jeff.

"You can do it!" cheered Dinky and Stan.

Egged on, Mr. Hughes got louder and wilder. When Christy finished, he bellowed, *"Yes!"* and turned his attention to Raymond. "Come on, Raymond! Last question! Fourth down, goal to go! Concentrate! Now, simplify the fraction! Time's running out! Five—four—three—two—you did it! *Touchdown!!*"

Mr. Hughes took off like a nuclear missile. Two mighty steps propelled him to the front of the class, and he spiked his clipboard football-style, throwing it hard against the tile floor. Springs flew every which way as the mechanism broke apart. Loose papers fluttered around the celebrating coach.

At that moment the door opened, and Mr. Doncaster entered the room. The principal watched the blizzard of papers settle at the feet of his newest teacher.

"Mr. Hughes?" he began. When Mr. Doncaster spoke, he kept his saucer-wide eyes riveted on the person he was talking to. Wiley and Jeff had awarded him the nickname Deer in Headlights because he always looked hypnotized, like a deer that had strayed onto a highway.

"Mr. Hughes?" the principal repeated. "What's going on here?"

Gasping, Mr. Hughes faced his boss. "We've just had a math quiz!" he puffed.

Still staring, the principal thought it over. "I see," he said finally. He took another step into the room, ushering before him a slender red-haired girl. "I've brought you a new student," he announced, casting the deer-in-headlights look all around the room. "This is Cassandra Levy. She's going to be joining your class."

Wiley and Jeff exchanged a knowing glance. To the nicknamers, a new student meant a new challenge.

Wiley opened his notebook to a blank page and wrote: *Carrot top?*

Jeff frowned. Not bad, but a whole lot more than hair color separated Cassandra from the average OOPS girl. There was a special spring in her step, a natural bounciness, as if she were walking on a trampoline and not merely taking the empty seat beside Wiley and Jeff. Also, she wore a full-length cotton skirt with a wildly colorful pattern of a circus parade. Jeff surveyed the classroom. Everybody else—girl *or* boy—was in jeans or khakis. Instead of the usual sneakers, she wore what looked like combat boots with massive rubber treads. Somehow, these were just right instead of big and clunky in Cassandra's tiny size. As she settled in the chair, she smiled at the boys and whispered, "Hi."

Jeff knew he should already have a dozen possible nicknames for someone so different—her little pug nose; tiny freckles like microdots! But all he could do was cross out *Carrot-top* and mumble "Hi" back.

"I think you're going to enjoy this class, Cassandra," said Mr. Doncaster. "Welcome to our school." And he left them.

Mr. Hughes mopped his face with a towel. "Clutch timing, Cassandra," he approved. "We were just about to go to the lab for science. All right, men, line up by the door."

In a body, 6B rose, and fell into two-by-two formation at the front of the room. Everyone looked back. Cassandra was still seated at her desk.

"Come on, Cassandra," the big teacher urged. "You're part of the team now."

The new girl's fair eyebrows were raised in an expression of confusion. "You said 'men.' Why are the girls lined up?"

Mr. Hughes laughed. "Oh, that's just an expression. You see, in football, you always call the players 'men.'"

"But this isn't a football game," Cassandra pointed out. "We're not a football team."

"Well, uh—" The smile was gone from Mr. Hughes's face. "I guess . . . uh . . . since I'm a football coach—"

"And none of us are *totally* men," Cassandra went on. "I mean, there are *boys*—"

An uncomfortable murmur went through the class. Who was this girl who had the guts to go head-to-head with Mr. Hughes?

The big teacher grinned sheepishly. "Well, this is your official invitation. Come and join the line."

As they marched down the hall, Wiley turned to Jeff. "You're right. Carrot-top doesn't say it all."

"Hey—" Charles poked Jeff's arm. He pointed in the open door of class 6A.

There sat Mike Smith, bland as ever, in the front row. His head was buried deep in a textbook.

Jeff rolled his eyes. "What about him?"

"You're not calling him Iceman," Charles whispered. "How is everyone supposed to pick up the new nickname if they never hear it?"

"Okay," groaned Jeff. He cupped his hands to his mouth. "Iceman," he said softly.

"Louder," Charles hissed.

"Iceman!" chorused Wiley and Jeff.

A pair of puzzled eyes rose above the top of the

book. Mike stared. Wiley, Jeff, and Charles were squeezed into the doorway, waving at him.

"Michael," came Miss Hardaway's stern voice from inside the room. "You'll have plenty of time to see your friends after school."

Mike, who never saw anybody before or after school, nodded. His face was a picture of astonishment.

"Iceman?" questioned Raymond in a rolling burp. "Him?"

"Everybody calls him that," Jeff offered dubiously. "It's—all over the school."

"Oh, yeah," agreed Wiley. "He's very cool."

Charles nodded his approval.

BIRDBRAIN

THE TOWN OF OLD ORCHARD, Pennsylvania, had never known two such close friends as Wiley Adamson and Jeff Greenbaum.

They had been born just six hours apart, and began life in side-by-side cribs in the hospital nursery. Growing up next-door neighbors, they had taken their first step on the same day. Wiley's first word had been "Jeff"; Jeff's had been "Wiley."

The two families had become almost one family because their sons did everything together. Wiley and Jeff team-mowed both lawns, team-weeded the shared vegetable garden, and team-ran every errand.

"I picked up an extra package of mozzarella," Wiley commented as the two walked home from the market with Mrs. Greenbaum's groceries. "Your mom's homemade pizza has been kind of naked lately."

"Good idea," Jeff nodded. "Did you remember to forget the broccoli?"

Zoom!

The two were about to step off the curb when a slight figure flashed by on Rollerblades.

Wiley jumped back, juggling the grocery bag. A carton of eggs popped out.

Jeff dove forward and caught it an inch before it hit the pavement. "Maniac!" he shouted at the skater.

Wiley squinted at her colorful skirt. "Hey, isn't that—"

Skillfully, the blader executed a hairpin turn and cruised up to them. Red curls spilled from under her helmet. It was Cassandra.

"Sorry about that. I was concentrating on the cars, not the people. You guys are in my class, right?"

"I'm Wiley, he's Jeff," Wiley said at the same time as Jeff was saying, "I'm Jeff, he's Wiley."

Eleven years of friendship had given them split-second timing.

"My folks put me in charge of unpacking my own

stuff," Cassandra explained, wheeling a delicate circle in front of them. "I opened the first box, and there were my blades, right on top. So I'm taking a break. My dad says I could be president if I wasn't so easily distracted."

"You just moved here?" asked Wiley, racking his brain for a nickname that went with "easily distracted."

"From Philadelphia," Cassandra confirmed. "My parents bought the property at the end of Farm Lane."

Jeff goggled. "You mean the old Gunhold place?"

"Right! My dad was sick of the city. He wanted us to get back to nature."

"That's . . . uh . . . great—" Wiley managed. It was going to be easy to get back to nature in the old Gunhold house. Nature could come right in through the broken windows and the leaky roof. It was simply the most ancient, run-down, shabby, unpainted, and probably haunted structure in all of Old Orchard. Rats went four blocks out of their way just to avoid it.

"It's a totally cool house," Cassandra enthused. "Of course, it needs a little work. But it's got so much character. I was telling Crusty about it in science. Neat girl, but what kind of a name is Crusty?"

"Oh," Wiley chuckled, "it's just a nickname."

"A lot of people have nicknames around here," Jeff

added. "As you get to know everyone, you'll notice—" He fell silent. Cassandra was gliding softly from side to side, her head thrown back, watching the clouds roll by. She was at least a million miles away.

The boys exchanged a bewildered look. Finally, Wiley reached over and tapped her on the shoulder.

She snapped back to attention. "Oh, I'm sorry." She grinned engagingly. "See? What did I tell you? Easily distracted."

"No problem," said Jeff. "Everybody daydreams."

"Oh, I wasn't daydreaming," she told them. "I was thinking about the blue-crested warbler sparrow."

"The *what*?" chorused Wiley and Jeff.

"Blue-crested warbler sparrows live in the trees near river valleys," Cassandra explained. "But with all the subdivisions going up around here, most of the trees get cut down. So the poor blue-crested warbler sparrows have no place to nest."

Wiley and Jeff weren't struck dumb very often, but this was one of those moments.

A horn sounded, and a sleek silver sedan whispered up to the curb.

Cassandra pirouetted and waved. "Hi, Dad!" She spun back to Wiley and Jeff, beamed, and said, "See you guys at school tomorrow," before skating off.

The circus parade on her skirt billowed out behind her.

Jeff frowned as she hopped into the car and disappeared. "The nerve of that girl! We're trying to be friendly, and she tunes us out like a bad radio station! I say we give Carrot-top a second look!"

"Or Birdbrain," Wiley added. "Did you catch that bit about the warbling sparrow?"

Jeff shook his head. "I suppose we shouldn't be so hard on her. The poor kid has to live in the old Gunhold place. I wouldn't board my dog there!"

"I wouldn't board my *gerbil* there!" Wiley countered.

"My *caterpillar*!"

"My *amoeba*!"

Jeff folded his arms and grinned in triumph. "I wouldn't board my *germ* there!"

"Good one," Wiley conceded. He offered up a high five, which Jeff accepted. And they hefted their groceries and headed off toward home.

chapter 4

NO HUSTLE, NO BUSTLE

MR. DONCASTER WAS at the bottom of the stairwell when he heard the commotion from above. Quickly, he ran upstairs and cast the deer-in-headlights gaze down the upper-grade hallway. Every single teacher was in his or her doorway, peering quizzically toward the end of the corridor. The door of 6B was shut, but the ruckus was definitely coming from there.

"What's going on?" the principal barked at Miss Hardaway, the 6A teacher.

She shifted uncomfortably on her four-inch heels.

Because she always teetered around on stiltlike shoes, Wiley and Jeff had given her the nickname Skywalker.

"It's Mr. Hughes's class," she replied nervously. "It started a few minutes ago. It was quiet, and all of a sudden there was this terrible yelling."

Grimly, Mr. Doncaster marched to the door of 6B and threw it open. Mr. Hughes was galloping between the rows of desks, gulping Gatorade, and howling like a madman.

"Make sure the ovals are filled in all the way! . . . Watch those quotation marks, men! They're killing us! . . . Find the main character! He's the quarterback of the story! . . . Who needs a trip to the pencil sharpener? *Break!*"

"What is going on here?" demanded Mr. Doncaster, screaming to be heard over the teacher.

Gasping and sweating, Mr. Hughes turned to his principal. "Shhh! This is the practice test for the State Reading Assessment."

"You've disturbed every classroom on this floor!"

"That's impossible," said Mr. Hughes protectively. "My team is very well behaved."

The principal pulled the teacher aside. "Not them," he murmured through clenched teeth. *"You."*

Mr. Hughes looked utterly bewildered. "I honestly

have no idea what you're talking about, Mr. Doncaster."

"You were yelling!"

"When?"

"Just now!"

"Oh." Mr. Hughes shrugged it off. "I may get a little excited on the critical downs, but I wouldn't exactly call it yelling."

"Well, I would," retorted the principal, "and so would anyone with ears!"

Mr. Hughes planted his sturdy legs like concrete abutments holding up a bridge. "If I'm going to expect my kids to give me a hundred-and-ten percent, I have to give them a hundred-and-ten percent in return."

"Next time try to be a little quieter about it," the principal said irritably. He focused the deer-in-headlights look on the class's newest student. "Cassandra, how are you settling in?"

"Totally fine, Mr. Deer—"

Wiley kicked her under the desk. "That's *Doncaster*!" he hissed.

Mr. Hughes glanced at his watch. "Game over," he announced.

"Game over?" echoed the principal. He looked around in alarm. "You mean time's up? But these tests are incomplete."

"I gave them the full half hour," said the teacher.

Mr. Doncaster marched up and down between the rows of desks, checking each paper. "But—but how do you expect to pass the real exam if you can't finish it? Peter—you barely made it halfway through!"

Peter chuckled. "Maybe it's because we're the Dim Bulbs."

The principal stared at him. "The *what*?"

"It's kind of a joke in our class," Christy explained. "We call 6A the Bright Lights because they win all the spelling bees and math contests. And we're the Dim Bulbs."

Mr. Hughes was appalled. "How did we get stuck with a terrible nickname like that?"

Wiley and Jeff sunk down low in their chairs, making themselves small.

Charles was looking straight at them. "Why don't you ask—"

Wiley leaped to his feet. "*Can I go to the water fountain?*" he bellowed, cutting Charles off.

Mr. Hughes ignored the outburst. "We're not the Dim Bulbs!" he exclaimed. "We're more like—the All-Stars! The MVPs! The Hall Of Fame, Powerhouse, Super Bowl, Record-Breaking, Legendary, Unbeatable—"

"You're yelling again," interrupted the principal.

"Sorry," mumbled Mr. Hughes, embarrassed. "I'm just a little surprised at this negative attitude. Men, we're every bit as bright as Miss Hardaway's team. We're all first-round draft choices."

"What you probably mean," translated Mr. Doncaster, "is that our sixth-grade classes are well-balanced. That's true."

"So how come the science fair winners all came from 6A?" asked Dinky.

"And don't forget the editors of the school paper," added Raymond.

"Stop!" Mr. Hughes held out a palm the size of a medium pizza. "It doesn't matter if you're in first place or last place so long as you give a hundred-and-ten percent."

"Last place certainly matters when it's on the State Reading Assessment," Mr. Doncaster corrected sharply. "It's the biggest exam we take all year. Mr. Hughes, I want to see these practice tests as soon as they've been graded." And he left the room, closing the door behind him.

Mr. Hughes mopped his face with his desk towel. "Time to hand in the papers. Come on up, men."

Cassandra cleared her throat.

"Whoops. I mean, men and Cassandra."

Christy stood up. "Mr. Hughes, if Cassandra doesn't have to be a man, I shouldn't have to be one either."

"All right. Men, Cassandra, and Christy."

"And me," chimed in Kelly.

One by one, all the girls in 6B spoke up for their right not to be men.

With a heavy sigh, Mr. Hughes perched on the edge of his desk. He looked very much like a normal-size person sitting on a footstool. "I apologize. I'm sorry if I offended anybody."

"Oh, we're not offended," Cassandra assured him. "We're just not men."

For the last period of the day, 6B went to the library to check out material for their research projects. Wiley's topic (gray sharks) took him to the same shelf as Jeff's (blue sharks). Peter was also there, looking for information on coral reefs.

He was still wide-eyed over the practice test. "Can you believe Mr. Huge *lied* like that? He told Deer in Headlights he wasn't yelling. He was screaming the whole school down!"

"I don't think Mr. Huge realizes how freaked out he gets," mused Wiley. "He coaches football, which means he runs up and down the sidelines cheering.

He has to yell to be heard over the crowd."

"And that's how he acts for a reading test." Jeff shook his head. "If it wasn't so crazy, it would almost make sense."

Mike Smith teetered around the high shelf. The tall boy was half hidden behind the stack of textbooks he was carrying. The top three volumes wobbled, over-balanced, and slid off the pile.

Peter stepped forward and caught the falling books. "Here you go, Iceman."

Mike stopped dead in his tracks. There was that name again—Iceman. He looked around to make certain there was no other possible Iceman nearby.

Crash!!

The stack toppled, and books rained everywhere.

"Sorry," muttered Mike, getting down on all fours.

"Here, Iceman," said Peter. "We'll give you a hand."

The boys from 6B stooped to help.

In a daze, Mike restacked his books. It was definitely true. For some reason, he was now "Iceman." Oh, sure, there were a lot of nicknames floating around Old Orchard Public School. But why him? And why Iceman?

As Jeff replaced a loose page, he spotted Charles Rossi in the next aisle. Charles was peering through a gap in the shelf, eavesdropping as usual. He wore a self-satisfied smile.

"Get out of here, Snoopy!" Jeff hissed.

The face disappeared.

Mike cast a feeble grin at Wiley, Jeff, and Peter. "Thanks a lot," he managed. And he left the library, tossing a haunted look over his shoulder.

Wiley stared at Peter. "Hey, Skunk, how come you called him Iceman?"

Peter shrugged. "I don't know. Everybody does."

"Everybody?" Jeff echoed in horror.

"Well—a bunch of people, anyway."

"But . . . but Iceman's what you call a *cool* guy," Wiley protested. "Mike Smith isn't cool."

"He might be," replied Peter. "He kind of is. He's laid-back."

"Laid-back?" moaned Jeff. "He's barely alive!"

"Well, anyway," Peter said vaguely, "he's the Iceman." And he went to sign out his book on coral reefs.

Wiley and Jeff were left bug-eyed.

"You don't think Snoopy's right?" Jeff asked hesitantly. "You know—that any old nickname could stick?"

"Don't be ridiculous," scoffed Wiley. "If that was

true, we'd already have so many names for Cassandra we wouldn't know which one to pick."

Jeff's eyes darted to the bright orange curls, bobbing up and down at the checkout desk. Even selecting a library book on the blue-crested warbler sparrow was a high-action event for Cassandra.

"Well, she's pretty new," he commented. "When we get to know her better, the right nickname will come to us."

Wiley nodded. "Let's pay a visit to the old Gunhold place after school today. We need to see Cassandra in her natural habitat."

Farm Lane was a rutted dirt road about half a mile from the school, just outside the town limits. All the other properties on it were small working truck farms with neat houses and well-kept grounds. But at the end stood the remains of Josiah Gunhold's Victorian mansion, a nightmare of turrets, gables, shutters, and chimneys. A symphony of peeling paint.

"To be fair," said Wiley as they approached, "it was probably pretty fantastic—you know, way back when it was new."

"Yeah, I'll bet it looked great in the Ice Age." Jeff shuddered. "I hope she doesn't invite us in."

"Don't be a baby!" snorted Wiley. "If Cassandra can sleep there every night, the least you can do is walk into the place in broad daylight."

It was like approaching a haunted house. The ancient wrought-iron gate creaked open to admit them into a front yard of knee-high weeds. They moved into the shadow of the old structure, and the temperature seemed to drop twenty degrees. They exchanged an uneasy glance.

Wiley nodded toward the porch. "Go up there and knock."

"Me? Why don't you do it?"

At that precise moment, a second-floor window was flung open, and a large bucket of dirty water was emptied out.

"*Heads up!*" cried Jeff.

The two hurled themselves aside just in the nick of time.

A mop of bright red curls appeared at the window. "Wiley? Jeff? What are you doing here?"

"Well," Jeff said casually, "we were in the neighborhood, and we thought we'd see how you were settling in."

"My mom and I were just doing some cleaning," Cassandra called down.

Wiley nodded. "I guess the maid has been goofing off since 1898."

Cassandra laughed. "Come on in, guys. I'll be right down. Not that way!" she added hastily as they headed for the front door. "The porch is all rotted out. You'd fall totally through. Go in the root cellar and up the kitchen stairs. There's a lot of cobwebs so try to hold your breath." She disappeared from the window.

Jeff turned to Wiley. "If we run, we can make it down the lane, and be out of sight before she realizes we're not coming."

"Just for that remark," growled Wiley, "you're going first."

Cassandra was waiting in the kitchen as they came up the creaking stairs, sneezing and spitting, and white with dust. She had shed her combat boots, but she was still wearing her school clothes. Today's long skirt featured a star map of the Milky Way galaxy.

"This is so cool!" she enthused. "My first visitors at the new place."

To their surprise, the kitchen was pretty nice—shiny plank flooring and gleaming brand-new appliances. But the hallway matched the rest of the house, with ancient buckling linoleum, peeling wallpaper, and dust, dust, dust.

"We're fixing it up one room at a time," Cassandra explained. "It's kind of my parents' dream. When I was growing up in the city, they always used to talk about a big old house far from the hustle and bustle of the rat race."

Jeff's eyes darted to the window and the field of weeds outside. "No hustle around here."

"Not even any bustle," added Wiley. "And the rats all take their time."

They looked to Cassandra, but she had tuned them out. She'd hoisted herself up on the counter and was swaying softly from side to side, her eyes tightly closed.

Wiley touched her arm. "Sorry. We weren't making fun of your parents' . . . uh . . . dream."

Cassandra flashed them a dazzling smile. "Oh, I wasn't *mad*. I was just, you know, thinking."

"About the blue-crested warbler sparrow again?" Jeff asked.

"Oh, no," said Cassandra seriously. "I was thinking about the Great Nicobar sand grub, whose only natural enemy is the dodo. And since dodos are extinct, there are so many sand grubs that the poor things can't find enough food."

"I guess they don't have Pizza Hut," Wiley ventured.

She laughed. "You guys are *so* funny. I can tell we're going to be total friends. Come on, let me give you a tour of the house."

It was two o'clock in the morning when Jeff rolled over and came suddenly awake. He stared into the silent darkness. The thought that had been nagging at his dreams became clear. He and Wiley had spent three hours at the old Gunhold place. Played four games of Endangered Species Monopoly! Not once in all that time had nicknaming Cassandra even crossed their minds. It was like they'd forgotten the whole purpose of going there! How could he have missed that? How could Wiley?

He climbed out of bed and looked out the window at the Adamson house.

Wiley's light was on.

HE'S LOSING WHAT'S LEFT OF HIS MIND

JEFF SMACKED A hard grounder to the shortstop. He raced down the line and dove into first base just ahead of the tag.

He stood up and dusted himself off. "How's it going, Snoopy?" he puffed.

Charles, the first baseman, glared at him. "Cut the Snoopy business," he growled. "I won the bet fair and square. Mike Smith is the Iceman, and you owe me a new nickname."

"The bet isn't over yet," snapped Jeff. "A week from

now no one will remember that the guy got called 'Iceman' a couple of times."

"I don't care about next week. I care about *now*. I win."

Jeff took a leadoff, then dove back to the bag when Stan, the pitcher, threw to first.

"I've got a few ideas for you and Wiley to think about," said Charles. "Last night I overheard my parents talking about what a great athlete I am—"

"You mean you were *snooping*?" Jeff cut in.

"I just happened to hear," Charles defended himself. "I was hiding in the stairwell."

Jeff hooted with laughter. "To call you anything but Snoopy would be a crime against science! You're a born snoop!"

"I am not—"

But then Christy got a hit, and Jeff was off with the crack of the bat.

Enraged, Charles forgot all about playing first base, and chased after him. "Come back here, Greenbaum!"

Jeff broke off the base path and kept on going straight into left field. Charles followed, shouting threats.

Wiley, the next batter, stared after them. "I have no idea how you score that," he commented. "This never happens in the major leagues."

"I think the runner's out," Dinky mused. "And the first baseman is—"

"Gone," burped Raymond.

Jeff and Charles disappeared behind the school portables.

"Well, we need someone to play first," Wiley decided, looking around.

There were no draftees nearby—only little kids, and a couple of fifth graders trading basketball cards. Except—

"Hey, Iceman," Dinky called to Mike Smith. "Want to play?"

The tall boy from 6A gawked. He had never been asked to join anything before. His first thought was that Dinky was talking to somebody else. But he had said "Iceman," and that was definitely Mike.

He took a step forward and hesitated. Maybe this was all a joke. When he walked onto the diamond everyone would break out laughing.

"Come on—uh—Iceman," sighed Wiley, shaking his head. "We need a first baseman. Help us out."

"Sure," Mike said cautiously. And when nobody snickered, he jogged onto the field and took Charles's place.

Gordon pounded his catcher's mitt and went back into his crouch. "Batter up!"

After the morning announcements, 6B boarded the bus for their field trip to Valley Forge.

They were barely out of the school driveway when Mr. Hughes began to rile himself up.

"Hit the turn signal!" he cheered the driver. "Merge onto the interstate!"

The man glared at him. "I got a driver's license."

"Sorry." The big teacher looked sheepish. "This is my first field trip," he admitted. "We really won the coin toss getting Valley Forge. 6A is stuck with the botanical gardens."

The driver glanced at the sky. Thick dark clouds were rolling in. "Not much of a day for an outdoor tour."

The rain held off through the nature hike. Then, halfway through the picnic lunch, the heavens opened up—not just a drizzle, but a drenching downpour that sent 6B running for the bus.

"Picture this, men," lectured Mr. Hughes, directing traffic with his half-eaten sandwich. "George Washington's army, wintering here at Valley Forge. And it isn't just raining; it's *snowing*! And they don't have great bologna sandwiches like these, and no nice dry bus to shelter in! And two years later, this wild-card team defeated the most powerful army in the world, and formed our country! See what can happen when you give a hundred-and-ten percent?"

A deafening crash of thunder shook the bus.

By the time 6B had finished their lunches, the storm was just settling in. Forked lightning slashed across the sky. Thunder rattled the windows of the bus, and the glass streamed with water. Everyone agreed that if General Washington's soldiers had to sit through this, they would have lost the Revolution.

At first it was fun to watch Mr. Hughes inhale all the extra sandwiches, washed down with gallons of Gatorade. Then boredom set in. Charles offered to arm wrestle all comers. Out of the whole class, only Cassandra managed to defeat him.

Then the top five arm wrestlers teamed up against Mr. Hughes's left hand. Cheers rang out in the bus, most of them from the teacher himself.

"Break my arm off, men!" he encouraged his opponents.

"*And* me!" grunted Cassandra, who was leading the group against him.

The laughing and joking turned to excitement as it became apparent that the five had a fighting chance against Mr. Hughes. Even the bus driver joined the howling spectators. In the end, Mr. Hughes's massive arm slowly overwhelmed the challengers. The ovation from winner, losers, and spectators was tumultuous. The bus seemed to rock until Raymond, in one massive rolling burp, announced that the rain had stopped.

6B stampeded off the bus and began splashing around in the sopping wet grass.

Mr. Hughes blew three sharp blasts on his coach's whistle. "Sorry, men. It's just too wet out here. There's no way we can have any of the activities after so much rain."

There was some grumbling, but eventually the big teacher managed to herd his class back inside for the hour-long ride home.

They drove along the narrow lane that fed the main road of the park. Suddenly, Cassandra leaped up and bellowed right in the driver's ear, "*Hit the brakes!*"

Shocked, the man slammed his foot on the pedal. The front wheels jolted to a halt, but the back end skidded on the wet pavement. It fishtailed out to the side, and the rear tires came to rest in the mud of the soft shoulder.

Mr. Hughes was on his feet. "Cassandra, what's wrong?"

Cassandra looked sheepish. "I saw that groundhog in the road ahead. I thought it might be the rare Pennsylvania needle-nose, which is an endangered species. But now I see it's just a totally ordinary woodchuck."

Shaken, the driver grimaced at her. "Okay, is the coast clear? I wouldn't want to run over any ants."

"It won't happen again," Mr. Hughes assured him. "Let's go."

The man put the bus in gear, and pressed the gas. The back tires spun in the soft mud, and sank deeper. He cut the motor and started over, this time in a lower gear. The engine roared, but the rear wheels did not climb onto the pavement. He tried a few more times with no success. The spinning wheels hummed a high-pitched scream, but the bus did not budge an inch.

The driver turned to face Cassandra. "You can tell your woodchuck friend to breathe easy." To Mr. Hughes he said, "We're not going anywhere. It's like bacon grease back there—no traction at all."

The big teacher looked worried. "What do we do?"

"We wait till another car comes by," replied the

driver, "and we send him to the main gate to call for a tow truck."

"But what if no one comes by?" piped up Charles.

"Then we ask the woodchuck to recommend a good hotel."

Mr. Hughes strode to the exit. "Open the door."

"It's three miles to the park entrance," the driver protested.

"Open the door!"

The teacher stepped down to the ground and marched purposefully to the back of the bus. There he braced himself against the rear bumper.

The driver stared into his side mirror. "What's he doing?"

Wiley gawked at his teacher through the glass window of the emergency exit. "If I didn't know better," he said in amazement, "I'd swear he was planning to push the bus!"

"Okay!" bellowed Mr. Hughes. "Give her the gun!"

The driver stepped on the accelerator, and Mr. Hughes put his considerable bulk into the back end, howling with the sheer effort.

"He's nuts!" gasped Charles. "He's losing what's left of his mind!"

"No, that's not it," said Jeff in awed respect. "He's giving a hundred-and-ten percent!"

"But nobody can push a bus!" exclaimed Christy.

All eyes were riveted on the heroic Mr. Hughes as he did battle with tons and tons of machine. And then there was a second figure out there in the mud of Valley Forge.

"Cassandra!" chorused Wiley and Jeff in amazement.

"I can't believe it!" snorted Charles. "She's as crazy as he is!"

Straightening her spiderweb skirt, the red-haired girl hunkered down beside her teacher and threw her slim back into the struggle.

Wiley and Jeff were out there like a shot, with Peter, Christy, and Raymond hot on their heels. Soon all the students, even Charles, were positioned around the bus, heaving with every ounce of energy they could muster.

"All right, men! Fourth and goal! *Hike!!*"

Miraculously, their combined strength moved the bus just far enough, so that the left wheel caught some traction at the edge of the pavement. The bus lurched forward and climbed up onto the road. As it did, the spinning wheels sprayed a shower of mud all over the students of 6B.

The slimy mess did nothing to dampen the celebration.

Mr. Doncaster hurried down the front steps of Old Orchard Public School to meet the bus. A rainy field trip was nothing new, but the day's thunderstorms had been so violent that he was relieved to see Mr. Hughes's class back safely.

The door hissed open, and out filed the students of 6B, twenty-five swamp creatures who would not have been recognized by their own mothers. Their faces were brown with mud, their hair was matted, their clothes dripped, and their shoes squished with dark slime. Bringing up the rear was their teacher, a mountain of muck so filthy that only his clear blue eyes identified him as Mr. Hughes.

The deer-in-headlights look burned like a laser beam. The principal's mouth fell open, but no sound came out. Finally, he managed to croak, "What happened?"

The bus driver supplied the answer. "We saved a woodchuck." Then he shut the door, and roared off.

chapter 6

KNOW ANY GOOD BIRD DOCTORS?

WILEY AND JEFF always met at one of their houses for breakfast before school each morning. Today the Adamson home was the spot, with bagels and orange juice on the menu. But the topic of conversation was the same one that had dominated breakfast for the last two weeks: a nickname for Cassandra.

"I still say we should concentrate on the way she can tune out the whole world," was Jeff's opinion. "Maybe Dizzy—"

Wiley shook his head. "Too negative." He took a

bite of his bagel and talked around it. "She's got those combat boots. Why don't we call her G.I. Jane?"

"Yeah, but she's more than a pair of boots," Jeff reasoned. "She creamed everybody at arm wrestling at Valley Forge. How about Miss Schwarzenegger?"

"Not bad," Wiley approved. "But it leaves out all that other stuff about her." He slammed down his juice glass. "Man, we've never had this kind of problem with a nickname before!"

"Why do you have to call her anything?" came the bored voice of Lisa Adamson, Wiley's sixteen-year-old sister.

"Butt out," groaned her brother.

"It's a legitimate question," she persisted. "Why does the whole world have to have a nickname?"

"It just does," groaned Wiley.

"All right," she challenged. "What's *my* nickname?"

"It's only for our school," Jeff said nervously.

Actually, Wiley and Jeff *did* have a secret title for Lisa: Soap Opera Adamson, or Soap for short. It referred to her love life, which Wiley and Jeff knew well. They had been there for most of it, spying from the bushes or hidden in the basement, usually doubled over with laughter.

Lisa smirked at her brother. "I think you have a crush on Cassandra."

"No way!" scoffed Wiley.

"Then why are you blushing?"

Wiley glared at her. "Shut up. Shut upper than you've ever shut up before."

"Leave the poor kid alone," mumbled Donald Briscoe, Lisa's boyfriend and lift to school. "Come on. Eat up. I've got an early football practice."

"Hey," said Wiley. "If you play football, you must know Mr. Huge."

Donald frowned. "Huge? Oh, you mean Coach Hughes. Sure I know him."

"He's our new teacher," Jeff told him.

Donald looked horrified. "They took a football coach and turned him into a *teacher*?" He snapped his fingers. "That explains why he's been acting so strange lately."

"He's been acting pretty strange in our class too," Wiley grinned.

"Tell me about it," sighed Donald. "He's too quiet, never gets excited, never breaks a sweat at practice. He's almost a zombie."

"Mr. *Huge*?!" chorused Wiley and Jeff in disbelief. Of all the words to describe the new teacher, *zombie* was last on the list. "*Our* Mr. Huge?"

Lisa downed her orange juice and stood up. "Ready."

As the couple left the house, Wiley and Jeff took their usual positions at the living room window. It was always a spectacle to watch Donald Briscoe operate a motor vehicle. He could back out of a driveway like he was racing in the Indianapolis 500. This had earned him the nickname Indy.

His car was an ancient Chevy Blazer with a raised chassis and monster truck tires. He reversed out into the road at breakneck speed, shifting gears with a gut-wrenching screech.

Whump!! A dark blur flew into the cloud of burned oil, and bounced off the Blazer.

Oblivious to the collision, Donald and Lisa disappeared down the street at sixty miles an hour. Wiley and Jeff ran onto the scene, waving their arms to clear the smoke.

"What was that?" asked Jeff.

Wiley was the first to see it. A small brownish bird lay at the base of the curbstone. Cautiously, he turned the victim over with the toe of his sneaker. "I think it's dead."

And then the feathers moved.

"It's alive!" cheered Jeff.

Stunned, the mysterious bird struggled to right itself. It certainly was a strange-looking creature. It was a dark mustard color, except for the top of its head. There, the feathers were a brilliant blue.

Wiley frowned. "I know this is crazy, but it looks kind of familiar."

Just then, the tiny beak opened and a faint sickly sound was heard, a sort of weak warbling—

It hit both boys at the same time. "*The blue-crested warbler sparrow!*" they chorused.

"That's where we saw it!" Wiley added breathlessly. "Cassandra's project!"

"She *loves* the blue-crested warbler sparrow!" exclaimed Jeff. "Let's go call her!"

"Not so fast." Wiley grabbed him by the belt. "This bird just took a direct hit from the Indymobile."

"All the more reason why we should call her right away," Jeff argued. "So she gets a chance to see it before it dies."

"Think," ordered Wiley, tapping his temple. "If we show her a blue-crested warbler sparrow, and it croaks on her, she'll be crushed. We've got to nurse this bird back to health. *Then* we can take it to Cassandra."

"You're right," Jeff agreed.

Both boys spent a long moment examining the tiny

patient. "Uh, know any good bird doctors?" Jeff asked finally.

"How about your mom?" Wiley suggested. "She's a nurse."

"Yeah, but for *people.* And besides, she's already at work."

"Well," said Wiley decisively, "we had a gerbil once, and Indy sideswiped it. My mom pulled it through."

Mrs. Adamson finished wrapping the gauze around the Popsicle-stick splint that supported the sparrow's broken wing. "There. That should do it."

Wiley scratched his head. "I don't know, Mom. I don't think he's going to make it. He can barely warble."

"He's more dead duck than warbler sparrow," Jeff confirmed mournfully.

"That should be his name," Wiley agreed. "D. D. for short."

"*He* might be a girl," Mrs. Adamson pointed out.

Jeff shook his head. "The ones with the blue crest are the males. He's a he, all right."

Mrs. Adamson looked surprised. "I didn't know you boys were bird experts."

"Oh, it's not us," Wiley explained. "We sit next

to the world's greatest authority on the blue-crested warbler sparrow."

"It won't help," Jeff put in. "I don't think D. D.'s going to be around for long." His happy mental image of presenting Cassandra with her very favorite endangered bird was replaced by a new, grimmer picture. It was he and Wiley burying D. D. in a grocery bag in the backyard.

"Don't be such a couple of pessimists." Wiley's mother laughed. "The poor little creature is just dazed and scared. When his wing heals, he should be just fine."

The boys lined a plastic laundry basket with a soft blanket, and placed the injured bird tenderly inside. They carried D. D. to the big toolshed that stood on the property line between the Adamsons' house and the Greenbaums' next door. Both families shared the shed, so the bird was being held in joint custody.

Carefully, Wiley set an old window screen across the top of the basket. "So he won't fly away," he explained.

Jeff laughed mirthlessly. "D. D. couldn't fly if you strapped a jet engine to his tail feathers."

As if on cue, the bird lifted its little blue head and managed a fairly respectable warble.

Wiley raised an eyebrow. "Maybe he's not going

to die," he said hopefully. "Maybe he's going to live."

"And get really strong," added Jeff.

"He'll be a professional wrestler," Wiley agreed.

"With big muscular feathers!"

"He'll use his superstrength to fight crime!"

"He'll be elected president of the United States!"

Wiley cackled in triumph. "And *then* we'll take him over to the old Gunhold place and show him to Cassandra!"

Laughing, they traded high fives over the basket.

Jeff grabbed his arm. "Come on. We'll be late for school."

They arrived just as the bell rang. There was a commotion in the halls. The school yard softball players were cheering and babbling. Ecstatic high fives flew in all directions.

A waving V-for-victory sign practically poked Jeff's eyes out. He escaped into room 6B, running for his life.

"Hey, cut it out!"

"What's going on?" Wiley added, mystified.

Peter burst in after them. "Where *were* you guys? You just missed the greatest moment in softball history!"

Raymond belched the word "Awesome!"

"If I didn't see it with my own eyes," added Christy, "I wouldn't believe it!"

Wiley stared at them. "A game we have twice a day, *every* day! What could happen?"

Kelly gave the play-by-play. "We were down by three, two outs, bases loaded, with the bell about to ring. And who comes up to bat? The Iceman!"

"What Iceman?" asked Jeff. His jaw dropped. "*Our* Iceman? Mike Smith?"

He caught a wink and a leer from Charles.

"Now I know why they call him the Iceman," Peter went on. "He's got ice water in his veins! He hit that ball so hard it's in China—the longest grand-slam home run in the history of OOPS! The Bright Lights carried him into 6A!"

"You see?" whispered Charles. "Iceman—it's sticking like Krazy Glue."

"One lucky swing." Wiley shrugged.

"Are you trying to welch?" Charles demanded.

Jeff sighed. "Look, we admit that something weird is going on with Mike Smith. But that's not the same as a true nickname—are you listening to me?"

Charles was leaning like the famous Tower of Pisa toward the classroom door. "Shhh!" he cautioned. "Do you hear that?"

Jeff frowned. "Hear what?"

Stealthy as a cat, Charles glided across the room and flattened himself against the wall beside the doorframe.

Wiley rolled his eyes. "He can't even stop snooping long enough to argue about being Snoopy."

Charles beckoned madly. "Get over here!" he hissed. "They're talking about us in the hall!"

Wiley and Jeff joined him at his listening post.

Cassandra wandered over. "What's up?"

"Our very first snoop," Wiley wisecracked. "Now I know what it's like to be Charles Rossi."

She laughed, but fell suddenly silent when she heard a phrase that could only have come from one person—*a hundred-and-ten percent.* "It's Mr. Huge," she whispered.

Mr. Doncaster was the other speaker, and the principal did not sound friendly. ". . . Mr. Hughes, this is very serious. The State Reading Assessment is how we decide whether or not a sixth grader is ready for junior high. And your class did horribly on the practice exam."

"They were all-stars!" they heard their teacher exclaim. "The league-leading, MVP, electrifying, Pro-Bowl, Hall of Fame—"

"Not now," Mr. Doncaster interrupted impatiently.

"I've never seen number-two pencils fill in ovals like that!" Mr. Hughes insisted. "You could *feel* the effort in the room!"

"Effort, maybe, but no results," Mr. Doncaster complained. "Your scores were nowhere near 6A's. Many were below grade level; all were unacceptable."

"*I* accept them," came the firm voice of Mr. Hughes.

"Well, you're the only one who does!" snapped the principal.

"If I thought that they weren't trying," the teacher said tersely, "I'd be the first one in there whipping butts into shape. But I'm not going to allow anybody to say my class isn't first string when I know they're giving a hundred-and-ten percent! Who cares about test scores?"

"Oh, nobody," the principal's voice dripped with sarcasm, "except maybe the Department of Education, the school board, the parents, and me! The real test is less than a month away. Get your class prepared."

"Good old Mr. Huge!" whispered Cassandra. "He's a total sweetheart!"

"Sweetheart?" repeated Charles. "He's the craziest teacher in school!"

"He's sure sticking up for us to Deer in Headlights,"

commented Jeff. "Why doesn't he just blame Mrs. Regan? She was our teacher until two weeks ago."

"Maybe he thinks he can light up the Dim Bulbs," snickered Peter.

"I hate that name," Cassandra said sharply. "Mr. Huge is right. We should stop using it."

"Mr. Huge is the whole problem," Charles accused. "Who can read and answer questions with a six-foot-five maniac bouncing himself off the walls? That wasn't a test. It was like—like feeding time at the zoo!"

"I think it's kind of cool when Mr. Huge goes ballistic," put in Wiley. "I've never had a teacher who cares so much about trying hard. You look at him sweating, and you can't help doing your super-best."

"He's like our own personal cheerleader," added Jeff. "Not even the Bright Lights have *that.*"

They heard the principal's angry footsteps tapping down the hall, and scrambled to get back to their seats.

STOP COPS

MIKE SMITH SNAPPED the lock on his bicycle, heaved his knapsack over his shoulder, and started across the playground.

Mentally, he began to count: one, two, three . . .

"Hey, Iceman!"

Well, that had to be a new record. It had taken only three seconds for someone to notice he was there. Until two weeks ago, it had taken eleven years before anyone noticed he was even alive.

"There he is! There's the Iceman!" Kelly and Peter and the usual softball players hustled him over to the ballfield.

The two captains immediately began arguing.

"I've got the Iceman.'"

"No way, the Iceman's on *my* team!"

"Stick with me, Iceman! Blow off this doofus!"

Mike still didn't have the guts to come out and ask if he could play. Yet now it appeared that no one would even consider starting the game without him.

"Iceman," said one of the 6A girls, "there's a party at my house on Friday night."

"Uh, that's nice." Had he just been invited somewhere?

"So what do you say, Iceman?" demanded one of the captains. "My team or his?"

"Uh—" Mike reflected that his new life was definitely a lot more fun than his old one. But choosing between so many friends had its stressful side.

Mr. Hughes bailed him out. "Huddle up, men—and . . . uh . . . et cetera! I mean—"

"Calling all Dim Bulbs!" finished Peter with a laugh.

The teacher silenced him with a stern look. "Calling all First-String, MVP, Superstar, Hall of Fame, Prime-Time Players! The pep rally starts in two minutes! Let's show some hustle! *Break!*"

"Pep rally?" echoed one of Mike's classmates. "For *what*?"

"For the spelling bee," called Dinky as he jogged off with the rest of 6B.

"A pep rally for a spelling bee?" The boy stared at Mike. "I'm glad we're not in that class, Iceman. Mr. Huge is a nut job!"

"It takes all kinds to make a world," Mike ventured shyly.

The boy slapped him on the shoulder. "Iceman, you amaze me. You always see the big picture."

"Come on, Iceman." The girl having the party was back. "We're going to be making nachos."

"Wow," commented Mike. He really wished she would just come out and invite him. Mike hadn't been to a lot of parties, so he wanted to make absolutely sure he was on the guest list.

She was thinking he was cooler than cool—showing interest, but never quite saying yes. Cool as ice, that Iceman.

Mr. Doncaster was hurrying past the gym when urgent whispering reached his ears. He looked around the hall in confusion. The classroom doors were shut, and the gym was empty and dark. All was quiet, except—

Just past the folded bleachers, a lone light shone in the equipment room. The principal rushed inside, expecting to shoo some of his older students back to their classes. Instead, he found four of his teachers hunkered down amid the mats and floor hockey sticks.

He cast the deer-in-headlights look at his staff. "Has the faculty room been relocated?"

Mrs. Chang, the librarian, chuckled. "Don't worry, everything's fine. We were just having a little unofficial meeting about your Mr. Hughes."

"He's crazy!" blurted Miss Hardaway. "He made us have a coin toss at the sixth-grade spelling bee!"

"No cheerleaders?" joked the principal.

Miss Hardaway was not in a laughing mood. "*He* was the cheerleader," she said feelingly. "*And* the halftime show. *And* fifty thousand screaming fans!"

"At least you don't have the classroom right below him," complained Mr. Richards, who taught third grade. "His footsteps are like thunderclaps! And when he gets riled up, he starts leaping around. Yesterday a huge chunk of plaster came off the ceiling and fell right in the fish tank. The algae eater will never be the same."

"I still say it's easier to *listen* to Mr. Hughes than to deal with him directly," put in Mr. Cordis, the science teacher. "Every time he walks into the lab, I cringe. Because pretty soon he's going to start cheering on somebody's experiment. And before you know it, the kids are all worked up too. It's only a matter of time before beakers are dropping, and acid is spilling, and somebody's notebook has caught fire from the Bunsen burners. And there's Mr. Hughes, galloping through the room, blowing his whistle—"

"That whistle!" interrupted Miss Hardaway in a haunted tone. "Sometimes I hear it in my sleep."

The librarian faced her boss. "Look, we've got nothing against Ted Hughes, and he genuinely seems to love his class. But he just can't leave his coaching on the football field."

The principal nodded. "I've spoken to the man about it. He won't even admit he has a problem."

"I think he gets so excited that he doesn't really notice how disruptive he is," offered Mr. Cordis.

"Come off it," scoffed Mr. Richards. "That would be like not noticing a train wreck."

"A train wreck would be soft and soothing music compared with Ted Hughes at a spelling bee," Miss Hardaway said honestly. "I didn't have the nerve to ask him for two kids to take over Safety Patrol this afternoon. I just wanted him out of my class!"

Mr. Doncaster sighed. "I'll look after that." He dropped his voice to a whisper. "It's possible that

Mr. Hughes won't be here forever. 6B did very badly on the practice test for the State Reading Assessment. Most of the students didn't finish. I don't think they can concentrate when he's around."

Miss Hardaway rolled her eyes. "I wonder why."

Mrs. Chang nodded. "He belongs on a football field—big, open, outdoors. Face it, Ted Hughes is too *loud* for a small classroom!"

When Mr. Doncaster walked into room 6B at the end of the day, he found the teacher and his students crouched over in a tight circle.

"Mr. Hughes, what on earth are you doing? Did someone lose a contact lens?"

Mr. Hughes laughed. "We're huddling. It's a great way to pass out the homework and go over the game plan for tomorrow."

The deer-in-headlights look was intense.

"I see," said the principal. "Well, I have an announcement."

"Sure. Huddle up," Mr. Hughes invited. "Come on, men. Make room for Mr. Doncaster."

"And girls," added Cassandra as they shuffled.

"Uh—thank you, no," said the principal.

Mr. Hughes seemed disappointed. "Okay, *break.*"

The huddle dissolved, and the students took their seats.

The deer-in-headlights eyes surveyed the room. "I wanted to let everyone know that the sixth-grade Thanksgiving party is going to be a Sadie Hawkins dance this year." He added, "That means the girls invite the boys."

"Actually, Mr. Doncaster," put in Cassandra, "girls can ask guys out any time they want. In nature, there are many species where the female is in charge of the courting ritual."

Peter reached over and nudged Jeff. "Hey, which one of you guys do you think Cassandra's going to ask to the dance?"

Jeff looked surprised. "What makes you think she'll ask one of us?" But before the question was out of his mouth, he knew the answer. She was new in town; he and Wiley were the only friends she'd made so far. Of course it would be one of them.

Jeff didn't know how to dance. But Cassandra would probably make it kind of cool. She'd wear one of those wacked-out skirts of hers. And combat boots.

His brow clouded. Of course, she might ask Wiley. . . .

"One more thing," the principal was saying. "Miss

Hardaway's class will be at the botanical gardens this afternoon, so I'll need two students to take over Safety Patrol."

"No problem, sir." Mr. Hughes glanced at the top of his class list. "Wiley Adamson and—"

"I'll do it," Cassandra piped up.

"Fine. Wiley and Cassandra."

On Safety Patrol, Cassandra Levy was an amazmg sight. Her bright orange fluorescent vest almost perfectly matched her brilliant red hair, and she had added a pair of glittery rhinestone sunglasses. Her long skirt depicted a field of daffodils with a gold sequin for the head of each flower. She had switched her boots for Rollerblades. As she glided back and forth across Main Street, guiding the OOPS students, she sparkled like a starburst on wheels.

Jeff watched from behind the flagpole. He had a stomachache. Not the Alka Seltzer variety. This was the kind that came from being left out.

Left out of what? Safety Patrol? He and Wiley had always made fun of the kids who volunteered, nicknaming them Stop Cops because of the signs they carried.

Cassandra's sharp green eyes locked in on him. "Hi,

Jeff! Need any help crossing the street?" she joked.

Grinning, he marched down to the curb. "Too bad you got drafted for Stop Cops," he told Wiley sympathetically.

Instead of complaining, Wiley held up his sign and hauled Jeff out into the crosswalk.

Jeff shook himself free. "I'm not ready to go home yet."

Wiley stared at him. "It's three-thirty. What are you staying for—the laser light show?"

The stomachache was getting worse. "Maybe you guys need some help."

"Oh, no thanks," replied Wiley blandly.

Cassandra executed a spinning jump in the road.

"It's no problem," Jeff persisted. "Here, let me hold your sign for a while."

"*No!*" snapped Wiley. Then, in his normal voice, "I mean, you're not wearing a vest. It's against the traffic laws for you to have a sign."

"I'd better stay," Jeff decided. "You know—just in case it gets busy again."

Cassandra wheeled by in a backward figure eight. "Everybody's gone," she reported.

"I'll stay anyway," said Jeff through clenched teeth.

"It's *not necessary*," insisted Wiley.

"Yes, it is."

"No, it's not."

They were still arguing this point when Mr. Doncaster pulled out of the parking lot, and rolled down his window to send them home.

"It's crooked," said Donald Briscoe.

"It's perfectly straight," Lisa insisted. "Start hammering."

Donald began to pound the nail into the wood-paneled wall of the Adamsons' family room.

Wiley wandered in to investigate the noise. He watched his sister's boyfriend hang up the Old Orchard High School football team picture.

"It's crooked," Wiley commented.

"No, it isn't," Lisa insisted.

"I knew it!" Donald exclaimed. "It's tilted to the left."

Wiley frowned. "I think it's tilted to the right."

Lisa rolled her eyes. "Let's ask Jeff. Where is he?"

Wiley shrugged. "How should I know?"

Lisa was surprised. "You mean he's not here?"

Wiley stuck his jaw out stubbornly. "Why should he be?"

"Because he's here more than I am!" Lisa snapped.

"Mom saw him out by the shed feeding D. D.," Wiley reported. "He's sulking because he didn't get to be on Safety Patrol with me."

"Safety Patrol?" Lisa repeated. "You've never volunteered for anything since the day you were born. And neither has Jeff."

Donald stepped back from the picture. "Hey, Wiley, can you pick out which one is me? I'll give you a hint: I'm two helmets behind the backup punter."

Wiley examined the photograph. "Where's Mr. Huge?"

"Oh, he quit," Donald replied. "He said he couldn't give a hundred-and-ten percent to the team without shortchanging his class. Didn't he tell you?"

"Maybe he just told Jeff." Lisa smirked. "And Jeff gave the news to D.D. and said 'pass it on.'"

But Wiley had already left the room with his hands over his ears.

MARATHON

MR. DONCASTER WAS washing his hands in the downstairs boys' bathroom when Mr. Richards entered. The principal cast the deer-in-headlights look at the wire fishnet the third-grade teacher held in his hand. In the mesh lay an unmoving gray form.

"My algae eater," the teacher explained mournfully. "He died of complications from when Hughes rained half my ceiling into the fish tank. I'm giving him a burial at sea." He stepped into the corner stall and emerged a moment later with an empty net.

The principal dried his hands with a paper towel. "Well, I can't help your fish, but it might cheer you up to know that our problems with Mr. Hughes are nearly over."

Mr. Richards raised an eyebrow. "Really?"

Mr. Doncaster nodded. "He'll be back on the football field by Christmas. The superintendent was so appalled by 6B's practice test that he gave me the go-ahead to start interviewing new teachers. Let me tell you who I'm thinking of. . . ."

The two men walked out together. A moment later a round face peered out from the center stall. It was Charles Rossi, alias Snoopy.

The students of 6B were settling into their seats when Charles came charging through the door. Purple and breathless, he ran up to Wiley and Jeff.

"Go away, Snoopy," said Wiley, shuffling notebooks. "The bet's off."

Frantically, Charles flapped his arms and moved his lips. But no sound came out.

"Forget it," Jeff advised. "We know what you're trying to say, and the answer is no."

Finally, Charles managed to suck up enough air to rasp, "Mr. Huge is getting fired!"

Silence fell over the room like a drape on a birdcage.

"How could you know that?" demanded Jeff.

But no reply was needed. The CIA didn't gather information as efficiently as Charles Rossi.

"It's not fair!" wailed Cassandra. "The other teachers don't understand how great he is! They just see that he's big and loud and different—that he doesn't fit in!"

"It must be tough to fit in when you're Mr. Huge," mused Jeff. "Except to fit in—you know—an aircraft hangar."

"Or a football team," added Raymond. "Maybe he asked to go back to the high school."

"Wait a second!" All at once, Wiley remembered Donald's team picture. "Indy told me Mr. Huge *quit* the football team! If he gets fired from OOPS, he's out of a job!"

"We've got to save Mr. Huge!" Cassandra gasped.

"How?" countered Gordon. "Deer in Headlights is the principal. It's not up to us."

Jeff's brow furrowed. "Well, what did Mr. Huge do to get in so much trouble?"

Peter stared at him. "What *didn't* he do? Yell the school down, sweat up the world—"

"Yeah, but there's got to be *one* thing that put it over the top," Wiley interrupted. "Snoopy, did Deer in Headlights give any reason *why* they're getting rid of Mr. Huge?"

Charles thought back. "He said something about how bad we all did on that practice reading test."

"Aha!" Cassandra was triumphant. "The real test isn't for three weeks. If we all do *awesome*, I'll bet Mr. Huge can stay!"

"Aren't you forgetting something?" Peter cut in. "We didn't flub that test because of bad weather, you know. We're lousy at English. Maybe—" He paused thoughtfully. "Maybe we really *are* the Dim Bulbs."

"Yeah, right," chuckled Wiley.

No one else laughed.

Jeff looked around in concern. "Hey, guys, wait! You don't really *believe* . . ."

His voice trailed off. The students of 6B stood in embarrassed silence, their heads hanging.

Wiley and Jeff shared a guilty glance. Bright Lights and Dim Bulbs had come from them. Were the nicknames backfiring?

Cassandra's normally fair cheeks flamed red. "This has gone on long enough!" she cried. "It's okay to have a nickname for *fun*. But you can't let it tell you who you are! If I put broccoli in a jar, and stick on a label that says M&Ms, does that make it candy?"

"Is that a question on the reading test?" Peter asked suspiciously.

"We are *not* dim," Cassandra said through clenched teeth. "We're going to study our brains out and *ace* the State Reading Assessment!"

"We don't have anything to study," Jeff pointed out. "No practice questions, no shortcut hints. Nothing."

"We've got everything we need," Cassandra insisted.

They just stared at her.

"It's so obvious!" she persisted. "It's a *reading* test!" She pointed to the shelves at the back of the room. "We've got books in the class, books at home; there are zillions in the media center, zillions more in the public library! How do you get ready for a reading test? By *reading*!"

"Reading?!" chorused half a dozen voices.

"Think!" ordered Cassandra. "If you play basketball, and you want to be a better foul shooter, what do you do? You take free throws—over and over and over. Well, that's how you get better at reading—by doing it!"

"You mean, like, *extra* reading?" asked Raymond.

"I don't know any books," complained Christy.

There was general agreement.

Wiley snapped his fingers. "Mrs. Chang! She knows every book on the planet!"

There was an uneasy murmur.

Finally, Stan piped up, "Do sports books count?"

"Totally!" Cassandra crowed. "*All* books count. You can read the ingredients off a cereal box, so long as you read. And you don't have to answer questions or do book reports. It's just reading, period."

"I've had a lot of teachers," Peter said thoughtfully. "But Mr. Huge is the only one who can push a bus."

"I never got excited about school until I saw him in action," put in Dinky. "He's so psyched that you can't help getting caught up in it, too."

"He always sticks up for us," added Stan. "I guess it's time to return the favor."

"I'm in," sighed Kelly.

"I read a book once," mused Raymond. "It wasn't so ba-a-ad."

One by one, the students of 6B pledged themselves to a reading marathon for the sake of their teacher.

"One last thing," Cassandra added. "We can't tell Mr. Huge."

"Good idea," Wiley nodded fervently. "That guy could sweat up the North Pole. If he knew his job was on the line, he might drown us all!"

* * *

When Mr. Hughes entered his classroom at nine o'clock, he found no laughing conversations, no baseball cards, no spitball wars—in fact, there were no sounds at all. Instead, the big teacher was greeted by the sight of twenty-five tops of heads. Twenty-five noses were buried in twenty-five books.

"Good morning, men."

Nobody looked up.

"Those must be MVP books."

"Mmmm," came a few absent murmurs. Most of the class ignored him.

Mr. Hughes popped his whistle into his mouth and blew an earsplitting blast. The students of 6B were lifted three inches off their chairs. By the time they came back to earth, he had everyone's attention.

But it happened again. As soon as Wiley finished his fractions worksheet, out came his copy of *The Great Brain*. Now Jeff was reading, too. And Cassandra. As soon as the students completed their work, the books reappeared.

Mr. Hughes was bewildered. Since when was 6B such a bunch of bookworms?

Peter went to the washroom. When he came back,

he had obviously made a side trip to the library. His arms were laden with novels.

"Hold it." The big teacher stopped him at the door. "What are you, the Bookmobile?"

"Oh, ha-ha," Peter gurgled. "I thought I'd sign out a few extras. You know, just in case the books we have are too boring or something."

"This is a little bit sudden," observed Mr. Hughes. "Why all this reading?"

"It's fun," Cassandra supplied.

"I agree," said Mr. Hughes. "But it was fun yesterday, too, and nobody was doing it."

The bell rang for recess. In the teachers' room, Mr. Hughes was too confused to take more than a sip from his Gatorade. What was going on with his class? Were they pulling some kind of quarterback sneak on him? He gazed out the window. In the school yard, the usual games of softball, jump rope, and tag were in full swing. But not a single 6B student was playing. They were all draped in various poses against the building and along the fence, reading.

Mrs. Chang sat down beside him at the window. "I've got to hand it to you, Ted. Your new novel study certainly has the kids enthralled."

Mr. Hughes looked blank. "What new novel study?"

"That's why I was late getting down here," the librarian explained. "A dozen of them showed up looking for books. They're cleaning me out!"

"We're not doing a novel study," Mr. Hughes said honestly. "It just sort of happened. All of a sudden, the whole class went book crazy. I mean, yesterday I assigned a paragraph, and they acted like I was asking them to kick a hundred-yard field goal. And today—" He gestured toward the window. "I don't know what to do."

Mrs. Chang laughed. "Do? Get down on your knees and give thanks! If there's one thing that never happens enough, it's reading for the plain fun of it. Do nothing! Just enjoy it!"

THE ROLLERBLADING LESSON

"**IF YOU MESS UP** those Rollerblades, the store's going to make you buy them!" Lisa Adamson shouted out the window of her boyfriend's Blazer.

Wiley was just barely keeping his balance as he attempted to roll from Sports World across the uneven pavement to the car. "Mom and Dad said I could buy Rollerblades with my birthday money if I want," he managed. His eyes never left the sidewalk and his unsteady feet. "Well, how could I know that if I've never tried them?"

Like a man overboard clinging to a rope ladder, he clamped onto the door handle and hauled himself into the back of the Blazer.

Donald regarded him in the rearview mirror. "You're not going to get a great tryout in the backseat of my car."

"Oh, I'm going to skate," Wiley assured him. "I'm just looking for the right spot."

"Like where?"

Wiley made a big show of shrugging his shoulders. "Drive around a little. I'll know it when I see it."

"This makes twice in the same week that you've been sighted without your Siamese twin," Lisa commented as they squealed into traffic. "You're not getting a life, are you?"

"Jeff has a doctor's appointment, like it's any of your business," Wiley muttered. Suddenly he sat bolt upright. "Hold it! Stop right here!"

"We're in the middle of the intersection!" Donald protested. But he managed to screech to the curb.

"You're weird!" Lisa exclaimed. "What's so special about here?" Her eyes fell on the red-haired girl who was blading toward them on the other side of the street, long skirt billowing. "So that's it! It's that girl you like, right? Cassandra?"

"Shut up!" Wiley was struggling to get out the door.

"Hey! *Hey!*" cried Donald. "You don't have to crush me! I'll move the seat!"

"As soon as I'm out," Wiley instructed as he climbed over Donald, "drive away fast! I don't want her to see you!"

"It must be true love," sang out Lisa. *"Wiley and Cassandra, sitting in a tree, K-I-S-S-I-N-G—"*

"Shut *up*!" hissed Wiley. He popped out of the Blazer like a champagne cork, and hit the pavement rolling.

"Be careful!" shrieked Lisa. "If you get killed, I'm going to wind up grounded!"

Stiff-legged and frightened to death, Wiley swerved out in front of Cassandra. She swooped skillfully around him, and skated backward, keeping pace as he struggled along.

"Hey, Wiley, why didn't you tell me you're a blader?"

She looked genuinely delighted to see him. He didn't have the heart to tell her he was a beginner in grave danger of breaking every bone in his body.

"Oh, sure," he blustered, scrambling along. "I

haven't done it in a while, on account of my knee injury. And I've outgrown my skates, so my feet hurt. And my ankles—"

Cassandra grabbed his arm as he stumbled over a twig. "You're doing fine," she encouraged. "This is so awesome! We can blade together. It's the *perfect* break when you're reading all the time; you get fresh air and exercise. I do it every day."

"Me, too," panted Wiley. "I mean, you know, *before.*"

"It's so relaxing, too," Cassandra continued, whirling around him. "I get my total best thinking done. Right before I saw you I was thinking about the purple-back swamp alligator, poor thing."

"Why?" puffed Wiley. "Are they endangered?" Picking up speed alongside the traffic, he was feeling pretty endangered himself.

"Oh, no," she replied. "There are zillions of them. And everybody hates them because who likes alligators? But the purple-back swamp alligator is completely toothless, and eats only tiny swamp organisms. It's a bum rap for a sweet animal."

"But you still like the blue-crested warbler sparrow, too, right?" asked Wiley, thinking of D. D. in the shed at home. "Isn't that your favorite endangered species?"

"Oh, it's not endangered," she replied airily. "It's in

danger of being endangered—hey, you've got to use your brake going downhill!"

A gap was opening up between the two skaters as Wiley accelerated. His scared face snapped back to her. "Brake?"

"Your heel!" Cassandra called. "Use your heel!"

"For wha-a-a-a-at?!"

And he was gone down the slope, passing cars, his body locked in a rigid upright position. His anguished cry for help trailed behind him like a streamer.

"Get out of the way! *Get out of the way!*"

A pack of little kids scattered as he shot right through their hopscotch game. Barking dogs chased him, but even they could not keep up. He rocketed through the bottom of the hollow, and started up the other side.

"I'm slowing down!" he mumbled to himself with relief.

Even so, his momentum carried him halfway up the opposite slope. In a split second, he experienced the pure joy of stopping, followed by the horrifying dismay of starting down again, this time backward. As he picked up speed, only one thought ran through his mind: facing the wrong way, he would never see the bus that killed him.

"Oof!!"

A blow from behind knocked him off his feet as Cassandra tackled him at the knees. The force propelled the two of them sideways. They left the road, flew over the sidewalk, and landed in a bed of pink petumas.

He lay dazed, his nose bleeding all over the Grand Canyon pattern on her skirt. Incredible, he reflected. This cute, wacky, amazing, sometimes frustrating, unnickname-able girl had very probably just saved his life.

"Okay, kiddo." Dr. Brodsky pulled the needle from Jeff's arm and applied the alcohol swab. "That should take care of the measles into the next millennium."

"Thanks, sir."

"You don't have to call me sir." The doctor smiled.

Dr. Brodsky thought Wiley and Jeff were the two politest kids in Old Orchard. He never knew that "sir" stood for "Sir Inge," a nickname he'd acquired for being the doctor who gave a shot for almost everything.

Jeff checked out at the receptionist's desk and opened the door to the waiting room. His jaw dropped. There, propped up between Cassandra and her father, sat a dazed Wiley. His nose was buried in a nest of bloodstained paper towels.

"*What happened?*" Jeff's first horrified thought was that his best friend had been run over by the Levys' Lexus. But then his eyes fell on the Rollerblades hung by the laces over Wiley's slumped shoulders. And he knew.

"Hi, Jeff," Cassandra greeted. "Do you blade, too?"

"No, I don't," Jeff replied sourly. "And neither does he."

Dr. Brodsky poked his head into the waiting room. "Okay, let's have a look at the stuntman."

Wiley got up woozily. "Coming, sir." He tossed a feeble grin at Jeff over their shared joke.

Jeff scowled back.

Wiley's nose wasn't broken, and the bleeding stopped after some cold packs. So Mr. Levy and Cassandra drove the patient home, and Jeff caught a lift with them.

The Adamsons were grateful to have their son returned to them more or less in one piece. Wiley was sent to lie down with his head back. When they were finally alone, Jeff turned on his best friend.

"You are low," he accused grimly. "The *lowest* of

the low. You're lower than those dirt-eating insects Cassandra worries about."

"I was just trying to learn to Rollerblade," Wiley protested nasally.

"On the Cranston Street hill?"

"Indy took me there! The guy's unstable!"

Jeff folded his arms in front of him. "This is me, remember? I know what you're thinking before you think it. Stop!" he snapped as Wiley opened his mouth to speak again. "I don't want to hear about how you did this so you could get nickname ideas. The only nickname to come out of this is 'backstabber,' and it's for you! You waited until my doctor's appointment, and you went Rollerblading where you knew Cassandra was going to be!"

"Well, what am I supposed to do?" Wiley countered. "Have myself frozen until you're available again?"

"You're supposed to be *reading*, not nosing around Cassandra," Jeff reminded him. "You're trying to get her to ask you to the Sadie Hawkins dance. I'll bet you told her about D. D., too."

"I did not!" Wiley defended himself. "Not till he's better. You've got my word on that."

"Your word plus twenty-five cents is worth a

quarter!" Jeff raged. "Pour water on your word, and you've got pure H-2-O! Your word in a sandwich equals two pieces of bread!" He fell silent, fuming.

"You left out how my word is worth all the great nicknames that we've thought up for Cassandra," Wiley offered timidly.

Jeff looked shocked. Then he snickered. Soon they were both laughing, and all was back to normal between them.

But now they could sense something else in the room. Something that had never before entered their eleven-year friendship—suspicion.

DIDN'T

THE MONDAY MORNING buzz in 6B was all about books. Plot lines were yammered from excited lips. Reviews were given on a scale of one to ten. Authors were measured up against each other like championship boxers. Every few seconds, someone would shout, "Yeah? Well that's nothing! In *my* book—" And another argument would start over which story was the funniest/scariest/saddest/most exciting.

Into this book-club meeting strode Mr. Hughes, carrying a large paper bag. "Okay, men—and Cassandra, girls, the whole bunch of you. I still don't understand your game plan, and nobody wants to show me the playbook. But it's pretty obvious that you're giving a hundred-and-ten percent. So I owe it to you to give a hundred-and-ten percent right back." He ripped open the paper bag to reveal an enormous volume of *War and Peace*, 1,700 pages long. "*Break!*"

Not only was 6B reading at recess and lunch, but a half hour in the morning, and again in the afternoon was devoted to DEAR (Drop Everything And Read) time. All spelling words came from books in progress. Social studies became historical fiction and books about other places around the world. They even tried to develop math problems based on different plot lines: *If Detective Shapiro can unearth three clues per day, and it takes twenty-seven clues to solve The Case of the Overripe Tomato . . .*

Throughout all this, Mr. Hughes read along with them, poring over *War and Peace* with such intensity that perspiration streamed down his face.

"He's got to be the only person on earth who can sweat from *reading*," was Charles's observation.

"Everyone's having a great time," Cassandra enthused. "Total nonreaders are finding out they like it. It's easy, it's fun, it helps Mr. Huge—"

"The question is, will it work?" asked Wiley. "Sure,

the reading is going great. But when the test comes along, will we get the right answers?"

Jeff lay prone on his bed, chin propped on his hands, poring over the chart he'd been working on for the past hour.

WILEY

1. sits next to her in class
2. times at her house: 1
3. was her gym partner for square dancing (3 days)
4. arm wrestled her at Valley Forge
5. went Rollerblading with her
6. worked on Stop Cops with her

ME

1. sits one seat away from her
2. times at her house: 1
3. was her lunchroom cleanup partner (20 minutes)
4. didn't
5. didn't
6. didn't

Jeff sat up and frowned at the paper. There were an awful lot of "didn'ts" on his side of the chart, and no "didn'ts" at all on Wiley's. Plus, twenty minutes of picking up garbage in the cafeteria didn't exactly measure up to three whole gym classes of square dancing.

Did that mean that Cassandra was going to ask Wiley to the Sadie Hawkins dance? Not necessarily. Actually, it had been pure luck that Wiley, and not Jeff, sat next to the empty desk that had gone to the new student; pure luck that the gym teacher had paired Wiley with her—it could have been Jeff; it could have been Skunk, or Snoopy, or anybody.

His brow furrowed. Of course, luck had played no part in the Rollerblading affair. That had been Benedict Wiley, the traitor. On the other hand, how was it Jeff's business what Wiley did with his spare time? This was, after all, a free country. And if it was free for Wiley, then it was free for Jeff, too. He had every right to seek out Cassandra's company for Rollerblading (too dangerous), arm wrestling (he would lose), square dancing (outside of school? Forget it!), or anything.

For instance, the Levys were trying to fix up the most broken-down ramshackle house in the world. Well, Jeff Greenbaum could go over there and offer to help them turn it into a real human dwelling. It was the neighborly thing to do.

And he would stick a big fat "didn't" on Wiley's side of the chart.

In the toolshed on the Adamson-Greenbaum property line, Wiley removed the screen and dropped a pinch of birdseed into the laundry basket that was D. D.'s home. "Come on, little guy. Eat something."

He was impressed by how quickly the blue-crested warbler sparrow got across the basket to his meal. It was the first time the little creature had shown the ability to move around with the Popsicle-stick splint on his wing. Wiley raised an eyebrow. Maybe D. D. wasn't such a dead duck after all. He had to tell Jeff.

He replaced the screen, left the shed, and crossed the yard to the Greenbaum house. He didn't even consider knocking before wandering in the kitchen door. He was just as much a son there as he was in his own home.

"Hi, Mom-Baum," he greeted Mrs. Greenbaum. "Where's Jeff?"

"I assumed he was with you," she replied. "He went out about twenty minutes ago. I think I heard him in the garage, getting his bike."

"Oh." Wiley frowned, his lips hardening into a thin line. There was only one place Jeff would go that was bike distance away—the Old Gunhold house.

Cassandra and Jeff, each with an armload of bricks, headed down the two flights of stairs to the main floor of the old house.

"It's so fantastic of you to help out, Jeff," said Cassandra gratefully. She stacked her bricks atop the pile in what was going to be the living room. "It'll look awesome in here with real brick on the walls."

High above them, Mr. Levy clung to a ladder near the roof, removing bricks one at a time from a crumbling chimney. As they came loose, he was tossing them into the house through a third-story window. It was Cassandra and Jeff's job to haul them downstairs.

"I guess you save a lot of money," Jeff commented, "by reusing your old bricks."

"Oh, no," Cassandra replied. "New ones are dirt cheap. But they're so smooth and perfect and boring. These weathered bricks are chipped and cracked and stained and wonderful. They're twenty times cooler. See?"

Jeff did not see, but he said he did. It seemed pretty obvious to him that you used your old stuff when you didn't want to buy new stuff. But it was something you'd expect from a family who had moved into the old Gunhold place when they probably could have afforded any house in town. "Hey, what's that noise? I hope it's not your dad falling off the roof."

"Oh, don't worry. Daddy's a whiz on ladders." She listened to the muffled banging. "That sounds like it's coming from the root cellar." She led Jeff into the kitchen and threw open the basement door.

There, still choking on the dust and spitting out cobwebs, stood Wiley.

Cassandra was delighted. "Hey, look, Jeff! It's Wiley!"

"I'm surprised to see *you* here," the two chorused.

"That was fast," Cassandra beamed at Wiley. "Jeff said you couldn't come because you were so far behind in your reading."

"Jeff is going to get his nose squashed in a really thick book," Wiley promised darkly.

So Wiley joined the brick-lugging team, and the work resumed.

The boys labored in sulky silence for a while, following the bouncing red hair and today's skirt—a pattern of fresh vegetables—up and down the stairs.

Jeff had pretty much accepted the fact that Wiley

wasn't going to get his "didn't," when he heard Cassandra exclaim, "Oh, Wiley, my dad says we shouldn't carry more than four at a time."

Jeff looked over his shoulder at his friend. Wiley was heading down the staircase with six bricks in his arms.

"Oh, it's okay," Wiley said airily. "I used to do some weight lifting."

"Oh, really?" commented Jeff acidly. "Was that before or after your Rollerblading career?"

He dropped his bricks and raced back up. There he loaded his arms with seven bricks. He headed for the stairs, flashing a dazzling smile at Wiley as he brushed past.

Cassandra stepped aside on the first landing. "You guys are totally unbelievable! Here's Jeff carrying seven bricks! And Wiley right behind you with *eight*!"

Jeff's nine-brick load was pretty heavy, but when he added the tenth it was pure torture. His breath came out in short gasps as he assured Cassandra, "Oh . . . this is . . . really . . . no . . . problem!"

Upstairs, there was a crash as Wiley tried to pick up eleven, and dropped them all. It was music to Jeff's ears.

Jeff struggled the rest of the way down, deposited

his cargo, and sprinted back upstairs. If he could somehow make it with eleven bricks, he would be the undisputed winner of the afternoon.

Upstairs, he found Wiley reloading.

"You don't have a prayer!" the two hissed in unison.

There was a moment of shocked silence. Even fighting, they were so close that their thoughts were the same.

"Just watch me!" snarled Jeff, beginning to fill his own arms.

There was the fast and furious clinking of bricks as they strove toward the magic number of eleven. Finally, each groaning under the weight of ten, they looked around for the final brick. There were none left.

"Last one," came Mr. Levy's voice from outside. A single brick came sailing in the window.

Wiley and Jeff locked eyes, and a silent message flashed between them by radar: *Mine!*

Both boys lunged at exactly the same moment. They collided like sumo wrestlers. But instead of the smacking together of two muscular stomachs, the crash came from the violent meeting of twenty bricks. Wiley went down, his armload flying in all directions. Jeff staggered back, but held on. His balance dangling by a thread, he hugged his ten bricks and squatted down for one more. There was a gasp from Wiley as Jeff grasped number eleven and slapped it to his pile.

Slowly, agonizingly slowly, Jeff straightened his legs until he was standing in the center of the room with his monumental load. His arms were on fire; the tendons in his neck felt like overstretched rubber bands. He took a step forward. His legs were numb. His ears rang, and he could almost hear the foghorn voice of Mr. Hughes cheering him on. He wondered if giving a hundred-and-ten percent would spare him from being found at the bottom of two flights of stairs, dead under eleven bricks.

"Hey, guys—" Cassandra appeared in the doorway. She took a look at Jeff's feat of strength, and her green eyes opened as wide as the *O* formed by her mouth. "Wow!"

Suddenly, Jeff could have carried those bricks up the side of Mount Everest and back down again. He had a vision of a new page in the chart:

ME	WILEY
1. lifted eleven bricks	1. didn't

Mr. Levy hoisted himself in through the window.

He caught sight of Jeff, rushed over, and snatched the bricks from his arms. "What's the matter with you? Are you trying to kill yourself?" He turned around to where Wiley had quickly picked up four bricks and was heading for the stairs. "Now, that's sensible. Way to go, Wiley."

Another chart entry popped into Jeff's mind:

WILEY	ME
8. did something sensible	8. didn't

ASK THE ICEMAN

THE OLD ORCHARD Public School newsletter, *The Student Post*, hit the stands during afternoon recess. While the paper was officially the work of the entire sixth grade, all the editors were from Miss Hardaway's class. But this time there was a feature from one of the Dim Bulbs of 6B—the Endangered Species Crossword Puzzle by Cassandra Levy.

"Hey," said Peter. "What's a seven-letter word for '*warbling blue-crested feathered friend*'?"

"Sparrow," chorused Wiley and Jeff automatically.

"Wait a second." Wiley snatched the *Post* from Raymond and flipped it over to the back page. Across the top blazoned: *Ask the Iceman.*

"Cool! It's the Iceman's column!" exclaimed Peter.

Dear Iceman,

I am a fifth-grade girl, and I'm having trouble with my so-called friends. They say they really like me, but I think it's just because my dad works at Tidal Wave Water Park and can get them on Dunk Mountain for free. What should I do?

Signed,
Used

Dear Used,

I don't know.

Yours truly,
Iceman

"What?" Wiley rocked back on his heels. "That's it? 'I don't know?' What kind of advice is that?"

"It's the *perfect* advice," Raymond argued. "Iceman wasn't sure what to say, so he admitted it straight out."

Peter nodded in admiration. "It takes a big man to confess that he doesn't have all the answers."

Wiley was getting annoyed. "Guys, doesn't this seem strange to you? A month ago, nobody even knew Mike Smith. Now no one goes to the bathroom without getting his advice first!"

"He used to keep a low profile," shrugged Peter. "Laid back, modest. That's the Iceman's style."

Jeff's heart sank. "So nobody thinks it was—you know—a hoax?"

"Some hoax," burped Raymond. He read the last letter of *Ask the Iceman.* "'Dear Iceman. Has anybody asked you to the Sadie Hawkins dance?' I'll bet every girl in sixth grade is dying to take that hoax!"

Wiley made a face. "Listen, Gasbag, if he's such an iceman, how come this newsletter is so boring? I wouldn't paper-train a puppy with *The Student Post.* Look what they think we have to know: *November Open House to Be International Night.* Yawn."

"Think of the kind of goody-two-shoes who signs up for that," added Jeff.

"Major losers," agreed Peter.

A horn honked. Mrs. Adamson was waving at them from her Honda.

"I've got an appointment with Sir Inge," Wiley announced, jogging toward the car.

"I'll get your homework," Jeff called after him.

"Don't worry," Wiley tossed over his shoulder. "Cassandra said she'll bring it over tonight." And he climbed in the car, leaving Jeff clawing pieces out of his *Student Post.*

* * *

For the rest of the afternoon, Jeff floated on the sea of possibilities. With Wiley at the doctor's office, *he* was Cassandra's automatic best friend for the day. It was almost a date—except the word "date" terrified him. Just thinking it made his teeth chatter and his throat close up.

But he had the ideal plan. With their reading marathon in its third week, 6B was quickly plowing through the entire fiction section of the media center.

"So," he said at three-thirty, "why don't we take a walk to the public library? They've got a much better selection."

"Jeff, are you crazy?" Cassandra looked at him like he'd suggested they storm the library with machine guns. "We can't leave now! Today's the sign-up for November Open House!"

He stared at her. "You mean *International Night*?"

"Of course! I can't wait to see what country I get to work on!" She fixed her green eyes on him. "You *are* going to participate, aren't you?"

"Uh—yeah!" Jeff said quickly. "Wouldn't miss it for the world. Only," he dropped his voice to a whisper, "I was just thinking—it's too bad Wiley won't be doing it with us."

"We'll sign him up, too," suggested Cassandra.

Jeff shook his head. "He wouldn't want that. You see, Wiley doesn't have school spirit like we do."

"Well, that's *terrible,*" Cassandra said disapprovingly. "That's like the Mojave Desert hermit lynx, the most antisocial animal in nature. And at least *it's* an endangered species. What's Wiley's excuse?"

"Don't be so hard on him," Jeff advised. "In fact, let's not say a word about this so he won't feel left out."

She beamed. "You're a great friend, Jeff. Even when he's being a total jerk, you always look out for Wiley."

Jeff followed her long flouncing skirt (a New York City subway map today) to the gym. He was amazed at how crowded the sign-ups were. He was particularly surprised to see Peter and Raymond at the end of a long line to work on Miss Hardaway's Canada presentation.

Jeff sidled up to them. "You said only losers went in for this stuff."

"Losers?" repeated Peter in disbelief. "The Iceman's here!"

Mike had attracted the entire sixth grade to Miss Hardaway's corner. In sharp contrast, Mr. Hughes stood about ten feet away. His massive chest and tremendous muscles obscured the sign on the wall behind him: *Mexico.* There was no long line in front of him. In fact, the 6B teacher was alone.

"Aw, poor Mr. Huge!" Cassandra grabbed Jeff by the arm and hauled him over to their teacher. There, the two officially signed on to the Mexico team.

Naturally, Mr. Hughes was overjoyed. As the three started discussing their plans for International Night, the big teacher began to cheer.

"We're going all the way!" he predicted. "We're going to give a hundred-and-ten percent to take Mexico to the Hall of Fame!"

"We might have to bump it up to a hundred-and-twenty percent," put in Jeff. "There are only three of us."

Mr. Doncaster had noticed the same thing. He pulled five of Mr. Richards's third graders out of Japan and assigned them to Mexico.

At first, the eight-year-olds were terrified of Mr. Hughes, but Cassandra pulled them aside. "Don't worry," she whispered. "He's a real sweetie."

"He killed our fish!" one girl accused, her lip quivering.

"Impossible," Cassandra assured her. "Mr. Hughes is like the Algonquin spotted bear. He may be totally humongous, but he's soft as a puppy inside."

TOGETHER OR NOT AT ALL

"HOLD ON, CRUSTY. Last paragraph . . . done!"

Wiley tossed his paperback onto the plastic tub of books in Christy's arms. "This makes eight novels—more than I read all last year."

It was Thursday, just a week away from the State Reading Assessment. Every day at three-thirty, a volunteer from 6B would return the class's finished books to the media center.

"What did you put in there, an anvil?" groaned Christy as she struggled out into the hall with her load.

"I only like the two-hundred-pagers," Wiley called after her. He turned to Cassandra. "Let's follow her to the library. I'll bet I can knock off three more books before the big test."

"Oh, you go ahead," said Cassandra. "Jeff and I have plans."

"*Jeff?!*" Wiley's face twisted. "Well . . . uh . . . could we make it a threesome? I mean, all we're doing is reading—"

"Oh, we're not reading today," she replied seriously. "We're making a piñata."

Wiley gawked. "Why?"

"For International Night," Cassandra explained. "Jeff and I are working with Mr. Huge on Mexico."

Wiley struggled to maintain control. "*Jeff's* on International Night? Jeff?" What was going on? Every year since kindergarten, Wiley and Jeff had avoided November Open House like a public hanging. "But—well, how about I help you guys out?"

"Now, Wiley," she admonished, "you should have thought of all the total fun you'd be missing when you asked Jeff not to sign you up. Oh, here's Jeff now."

As they pranced away, Jeff was smiling at Wiley with every tooth in his head.

Wiley folded his arms in consternation. He should have expected something like this after brick day. But it wasn't over yet. All he had to do was go to Mr. Hughes and get himself on the Mexico team.

"Sorry," the big teacher told him. "You see, when we didn't have enough volunteers, we recruited some third graders, and they've really been giving a hundred-and-ten percent. I'd love to have you, Wiley, but it wouldn't be fair to them."

"But isn't there *anything* I can do?" Wiley begged.

Mr. Hughes shook his head. "The little kids are doing the hat dance, and Jeff and Cassandra are making the piñata. We're full. Try Canada. I hear they're putting on a pretty big show."

Wiley didn't much care to be on Miss Hardaway's team. But if he couldn't work on Mexico, Canada was the next best choice. At least he'd be on the same continent as Cassandra.

6A was a mob scene. Canada was shaping up to be the main event on International Night. Giant flags of the ten provinces were being painted around the room, and the red and white maple leaf fluttered everywhere. Wiley surveyed the bustling activity. Surely somewhere amid the hockey sticks, snowshoes, and birchbark canoes there was a job for him.

He found Dinky and Peter making a fur-trading outpost of Popsicle sticks. "Hey, guys, where do I go to join up? Straight to Skywalker?"

"Nah, she doesn't know anything," Peter replied. "You're going to have to talk to the boss."

"The boss?" Wiley repeated.

"The *Iceman.*"

"Okay, Skunk," groaned Wiley. "Where's Mike Smith?"

Peter stood up. "Hey, Gasbag," he called, scanning the crowded room, "is the Iceman over there?"

"I thought he wa-a-as with you," Raymond burped back.

"The Iceman? He's in the art room painting the Northern Lights," called Kelly.

"Don't bother going up there," Dinky advised Wiley. "I know for a fact that there aren't any decent jobs left."

"Except for the horse," Peter put in. "You know, the one the Mountie rides."

"I'll do anything!" Wiley pledged.

"You don't want to be the horse," Dinky warned. "The costume is about a million degrees, not to mention kind of smelly from people sweating in it for so many years. And there's something fuzzy growing in the hoofs. Plus you have to carry around the Mountie. It isn't fun."

"I'll do it! I'll be the horse!" Wiley cried.

"Well, you can't do it alone," Peter pointed out. "It's a two-person costume."

A diabolical grin worked its way into Wiley's fair features. "When am I ever alone?" he chuckled. "Of course Jeff will be with me."

"I thought Jeff was doing Mexico with Mr. Huge."

"Nah, he hated it," Wiley replied smoothly. "He wanted to work with the Iceman." And he walked away, congratulating himself. In just a few minutes, he had taken Jeff from Cassandra's side in sunny Acapulco, and plopped him down in the frozen north as the back end of a horse.

When Jeff walked into the toolshed that weekend, he found Wiley sprinkling birdseed into the laundry basket.

"How's it going, D. D.?" Jeff said to the blue-crested warbler sparrow. He noticed Wiley's copy of *Old Yeller* atop an old milk crate. "Pretty good story."

Wiley nodded. "I'm almost done."

"The dog dies," Jeff informed him.

"Awww!" Wiley looked daggers at him. "Thanks a lot for spoiling the ending!"

Jeff shrugged. "I finished it yesterday. It was my tenth book. That's tied for the most in class." He added, "According to Cassandra."

Wiley looked up. "When did she say that?"

"Just now. She left my house about five minutes ago."

Wiley's face darkened. "Well, she's wrong. I've read eleven."

Jeff smiled sweetly. "The Dr. Seuss ones don't count."

"The number of books doesn't count anyway," Wiley told him. "It's the number of pages. And I'm way up over 1,500."

"I would have read more than that," Jeff countered, "if *I* was reading baby books with giant print, like you are. Pages are nothing; it's how many *words.*"

"Not if they're big, long, hard ones, like in all the books *I* read!" Wiley snarled.

"I would have read a ton more," Jeff boasted, "but Cassandra and I were busy making our piñata."

Wiley turned to the blue-crested warbler sparrow underneath the window screen. "Hear that, D. D.? Now Jeff's bragging about being a traitor."

Jeff also addressed the bird. "Tell Wiley I learned it while he was out Rollerblading."

In answer, D. D. let out a long warble. He flapped both wings, even the bandaged one.

"Look at that!" Wiley exclaimed. "I think he's trying to fly."

Jeff nodded. "I guess it's time to take the splint off."

It was a major operation. Soon their hands were pecked and bleeding. At last, Wiley had a firm grip on D. D. The bird shrieked in protest as Jeff carefully unwound the gauze from the Popsicle stick that held the wing in place. Wiley released the sparrow, and both boys stood back.

D. D. took three dazed steps and then launched off the floor like a missile.

"Whoa!" Wiley snatched the laundry basket and quickly trapped the bird. He waited for the beating of his heart to slow back down. "I'd say he's feeling better."

"Better?" Jeff echoed. "He's a World War I flying ace!"

"He's a supersonic pilot!" Wiley amended.

"A NASA astronaut!"

"An intergalactic space warrior!"

A month before, they could have gone on all day,

topping each other and laughing. But something was different now.

There was an uncomfortable silence.

"I know what's going through your warped mind," Jeff accused. "You're thinking that if you bring D. D. to Cassandra, she'll be so happy that she'll ask you to the Sadie Hawkins dance."

"If *I'm* thinking it, how come *you're* the one who's saying it?" Wiley snarled.

"*Together,*" Jeff said firmly. "That was the deal. We bring D. D. together, or not at all."

A HUNDRED-AND-TEN PERCENT

A HUNDRED-AND-TEN percent.

The words echoed through Jeff's head as he sat at his desk, writing the State Reading Assessment. Had their read-a-thon helped? The answers seemed to be coming quickly and easily, but did that make them the right ones?

A hundred-and-ten percent. That was all Mr. Hughes ever expected of anybody. The big teacher stood at the front of the room, his meaty fist jammed in his mouth to keep him from cheering. But Jeff could see the droplets of perspiration rolling off his chin, forming a small puddle on the floor.

Concentrate, Jeff told himself.

He snuck a look around. Heads were down, pencils just a blur. At the next desk, Wiley was completely focused on his test. Like he didn't care that the two of them had not said a word to each other since that day in the toolshed. Beside Wiley, Cassandra held her long hair back off the paper as she worked.

She was wearing her circus parade skirt—the same one she'd had on the morning Mr. Doncaster had introduced her as the new girl in 6B. It seemed like a thousand years ago that he and Wiley had first tried, and failed, to hang a nickname on this strange, yet fascinating newcomer. So much had changed since then. . . .

Oh, no! He was daydreaming when he should have been working! This was for Mr. Huge!

All around him, his fellow Dim Bulbs were giving a hundred-and-ten percent.

But would it be enough?

TRANSPORTATION

INTERNATIONAL NIGHT WAS set to begin at seven, but OOPS was teeming with students by five-thirty. They scurried through the halls like rabbits in a warren, putting the finishing touches on flags, models, and displays. Last-minute rehearsals for skits and demonstrations were going on in every classroom and corner.

In 6A, Mike Smith received a round of applause from his Canada teammates as he glued the final piece onto an all-toothpick replica of Niagara Falls.

At the back of the admiring crowd, one sixth grader wasn't paying attention. Wiley Adamson was keeping a sharp eye on the hallway, watching for the arrival of Cassandra and Jeff and the Mexico team. Wiley didn't want to miss the moment when Jeff found out that he was no longer Cassandra's partner, but now fifty percent of a horse.

The families began arriving shortly after six, and by seven, the gym was jam-packed. The buzz of excitement was electric as the parents toured the displays. These were laid out in a horseshoe shape opposite the bleachers. There was quite a large crowd at the kindergarten exhibit on France. A whole class of hyperactive five-year-olds in berets was handing out paper cups of grape juice representing French wine. Already several purple stains decorated the plasticine Eiffel Tower. Other popular features included the Great Wall of China (fourth grade) made of Dixie cups; the Sahara Desert (first grade), which was an inflatable wading pool filled with sand and toy camels and, strangely, a plastic stegosaurus; and the Amazon rain forest (fifth grade) done entirely in broccoli and watercress.

Wiley spotted Cassandra introducing her parents to Mr. Hughes. A brilliantly colored sequined sombrero glittered on her red hair. Wiley frowned. Jeff was right there on the scene, being greeted by the Levys like a long-lost son.

Wiley rushed over. "Hi, Mr. and Mrs. Levy. Remember me?"

Jeff stared at him. "What are *you* doing here?" he hissed through his giant fake handlebar mustache.

Cassandra beamed. "Look, Mom and Dad—it's Wiley! Did you come to see our piñata?"

Wiley gestured over his shoulder to the large Canada display. "I'm participating. I've got a really important job on the Canada program."

"Doing what?" growled Jeff.

"Oh, it's—transportation," Wiley grinned.

"Well, I find all this remarkably impressive," put in Mrs. Levy. "There certainly wasn't anything like it at Cassandra's old school in Philadelphia."

"MVP stuff." Mr. Hughes nodded proudly. "The kids have really put a hundred-and-ten percent into this."

The lights flashed three times. That was the signal for the spectators to take their seats. The program was about to begin.

"Well, I've got to get back to Canada," Wiley announced. "Good luck."

"You, too," called Cassandra.

Jeff said nothing. Wiley seemed awfully smug for a night when Jeff, and not Wiley, was Cassandra's partner. What was going on here?

The OOPS parents were a kind audience, determined to enjoy whatever they saw. They cheered the kindergartners' purple-tongued version of "Frere Jacques." They clapped along with the Dutch team's earsplitting wooden shoe dance against the gym floor. They pretended not to notice when the high priest of the Incas threw up, or when the lead yodeler's lederhosen fell down. And they genuinely seemed to love the second graders as British palace guards, bumping into each other because they couldn't see through their tall fur hats.

Some third graders were performing Japanese Kabuki theater when Miss Hardaway began circulating through her group for a last minute check.

"Okay, my loggers are here," she whispered, marking off the names on a clipboard. "My fur trappers, my Eskimo fisherman—" She stopped in front of Wiley. "Where's your partner? Where's the other half of the horse?"

Wiley shrugged expansively. "I don't know. I'm not even sure who it's supposed to be."

The teacher stood taller on her four-inch heels. "Well, this is just peachy. How can a Mountie ride half a horse?" She ran a manicured finger down her list of volunteers. "Jeff Greenbaum. Where's Jeff?"

Wiley pretended to look around the semicircle of exhibits. "Hey!" He pointed. "Isn't that Jeff over there?"

Miss Hardaway put her hands on her hips. "What's he doing in *Mexico*?"

"I'd better get him before Japan finishes," Wiley advised. "I mean, Mexico's up next. Once they start, he's stuck over there."

"I'll go. You stay right here," Miss Hardaway decided. "And be ready to get into that costume." And she clicked off, ducking behind the exhibits to avoid interrupting the Japan performance.

Jeff was standing at Cassandra's side when a claw-like hand reached out and grabbed him by the shoulder. Petrified, he wheeled, and came face-to-face with Miss Hardaway.

"What are you doing here?" the teacher hissed. "Why aren't you in costume?"

Jeff reached up to make sure his mustache was still attached. "I *am*!"

She stared at him. "A mustache for a horse?"

Jeff was completely bewildered. "What horse?"

The teacher began pulling him behind the exhibits.

With equal force, Cassandra hauled on his other arm. "Where are you going? We're on in a minute!"

"I think there's been some kind of misunderstanding," Jeff tried to explain in two directions.

Mr. Hughes stepped forward. "What's the problem here?"

"Jeff is supposed to be over with *my* kids!" Miss Hardaway whispered urgently. "I need him right away!"

"But he's on *my* team," protested Mr. Hughes.

"No, he's not! He's on mine!"

Jeff was horrified. "I didn't sign up for Canada!"

"Yes, you did!" Miss Hardaway waved her clipboard under his mustache. "You're on my list! See?"

Jeff gawked. There it was, in black and white: *Greenbaum, Jeff–horse #2.* He was a horse! A horse in Canada! It said so!

"But that's impossible!" Jeff quavered. "I wouldn't forget something like signing up to be a horse!"

"Mr. Hughes, we're on in thirty seconds!" Cassandra put in nervously. "What are we going to do?"

Mr. Hughes tried to be reasonable. "Couldn't somebody double up on Jeff's job?" he asked Miss Hardaway. "You've got a lot of kids over there."

"And they're *all* busy!" she rasped. "We've got the biggest show of International Night! I can't start juggling assignments now!"

Over the PA system, they heard Mr. Doncaster announce, "Our next presentation is from our neighbor to the south—Mexico!"

Mr. Hughes made a split-second decision. "All right, Jeff, go with Miss Hardaway. We'll cover for you."

"But—"

"Break!" the big teacher ordered. And by the time the word was out of his mouth, the applause had died down, and Mexico had begun. Mr. Hughes cupped his hands to his mouth and shouted, *"Ole!"*

Cassandra cued the music for the Mexican hat dance. The five third graders ran into the spotlight, gyrating around a giant cardboard sombrero.

In a daze, Jeff stumbled after Miss Hardaway. He was still stammering excuses, but he was so distraught that he couldn't finish his sentences. *"I don't think . . . I can't understand . . . I don't see how . . ."*

She marched him up to a bench behind the Canada display. There sat someone in the front half of a horse costume. "Now, get dressed!" And she skywalked off amid her Canada team, hissing, "Places, everyone! Places! We're on in three minutes!"

Frazzled and disgusted, Jeff stepped into the back half of the horse. To his partner, he muttered, "What a rip-off! I never signed up for this! I don't even know what I'm supposed to do!"

From the head, a familiar voice replied, "Just be yourself—a horse's butt!"

HOW DOES MY MANE LOOK?

"WILEY?!" JEFF'S CRY of shock echoed throughout the gym, throwing the hat dancers off their rhythm.

"Shhhh!" Miss Hardaway glared at him.

Wiley popped off the horse's head. He said, "*Ole.*"

For Jeff, all confusion cleared. The "misunderstanding" wasn't a misunderstanding at all. It was just another dirty scheme, courtesy of Wiley Adamson.

"You are *low*," Jeff accused, his tone full of loathing.

"I have to be," Wiley defended himself, "to get underneath you."

The two were distracted by a pure, clear voice rising up in the gym. Wiley and Jeff peered over the wooden cutout of the Canadian Rockies. The hat dance was finished, and Cassandra had taken over the microphone. Unlike the other students who had spoken tonight, she showed no shyness or stage fright. Her voice rang strong and true over the PA. Her sequined sombrero gleamed in the lights, but nowhere near as brightly as her long red hair. Wiley and Jeff were struck dumb.

"This is a piñata," Cassandra announced, pointing up to where the large papier-mache figure hung from a ceiling beam. "It is used in traditional Mexican festivals and celebrations. A piñata can be any shape, and is often made to look like an animal. Ours takes the form of the Yucatan cliff-climbing armadillo, which is not only Mexican, but also an endangered species. As you will see, breaking the piñata releases candy for all the children of the village."

Mr. Hughes came up behind her and tied a blindfold over her eyes. Then he put a yardstick in her hands, and pointed her in the right direction.

There was scattered cheering and shouts of encouragement as Cassandra began to poke and prod at the hanging armadillo. These turned to chuckles when it became obvious that the piñata was quite a bit tougher than it looked. Cassandra took hefty swipes, landing some pretty good blows on the armadillo. Still the thick skin would not rupture.

Mr. Doncaster stepped in to the scene. "What seems to be the problem here?" he whispered, fixing the deer-in-headlights look on the piñata.

"I guess Jeff and I made it stronger than we thought," puffed Cassandra, still hacking away.

"Keep trying," encouraged Mr. Hughes.

"Don't start cheering!" the principal warned him in an undertone. "Every parent in Old Orchard is here tonight! Let's just take down the piñata, and cut it open."

"No!" Cassandra was horrified. "It has to break so the candy can fall out for all the children of the village!"

The principal removed Cassandra's blindfold, took the yardstick, and pushed it into Mr. Hughes's big hand. "*You* do it. And make it fast."

"Wait! Wait!" Cassandra stood up on tiptoe, and placed her sombrero on her teacher's head. Then she stepped back to give him room to swing.

Whack! Whack! The yardstick sang as it whipped through the air. But the armadillo held fast.

Mr. Doncaster was starting to panic as he watched Mr. Hughes break into one of his famous sweats. "Well," he said hastily, "we did our best, but—"

"Mr. Hughes!" called Wiley from the Canadian area. "Try this!" A hockey stick came sailing over the row of exhibits. Mr. Hughes lifted a massive paw, and snatched it out of the air.

Silence fell as the football coach took a baseball grip on the hockey stick. The armadillo hung before him, unbroken and defiant.

"Come on, Mr. Hughes!" piped Jeff. "Give it a hundred-and-ten percent!"

That was all the teacher had to hear. With a mighty roar, six-foot-five, two-hundred-eighty-pound Mr. Hughes swung the stick at the Mexican piñata.

POW!!!

The armadillo vaporized, spraying candy to the four winds. Shocked, wide-eyed parents looked on as the airborne sweets pelted down on them like a hail-storm.

"*Ca-a-andy!*" came a high-pitched cry. There was a stampede from the direction of France. Thirty-five kindergartners swarmed the exhibits, scrambling after the fallen treats. They crawled under tables and ran-sacked displays. They scaled Mount Fuji in a single bound and flattened the Great Wall of China, chasing after the brightly wrapped candies.

Cassandra watched them in awe. "Wow," she breathed. "Just like the children of the village."

Mr. Doncaster tried to ignore the ruckus and keep International Night rolling. "And finally," he announced, "our last presentation honors our neighbors to the north, Canada!"

"Not yet!" Miss Hardaway hissed urgently. "First get these kids under control!"

She received the deer-in-headlights look in reply. "We've been here for three hours! Let's get this thing over with so we can all go home!"

Resentfully, Miss Hardaway gave the signal to Peter to dim the lights. A lone spot shone on the toothpick Niagara Falls. Christy, the narrator, began: "Canada, the true north, strong and free . . ."

"Hey, kid, get out of here!" Wiley whispered to a kindergartner who was searching for lollipops in the horse's head.

Miss Hardaway was visibly upset. After two weeks of hard work and rehearsal, she felt it was unfair for all their efforts to be wasted. The gym resounded with the shrieks of the five-year-olds. Parents rushed around the exhibits trying to corral their little ones.

The rest of the audience was bored and tired. A few families were already heading for the exits.

But the show must go on. The hockey players slid around on stocking feet, the lumberjacks cut down cardboard trees, and the railroad workers pushed the line through the wooden Rockies. Miss Hardaway scanned the bleachers. Surely even a restless audience couldn't help but appreciate their grand finale—the Royal Canadian Mounted Policeman on his trusty steed.

Peter came rushing over to Wiley and Jeff, ripping off his hockey helmet. "Skywalker says to get ready *this instant*! It's time for the big finish!"

"Yeah, okay, Skunk." Wiley put on the horse's head. "How does my mane look?"

"Who's the Mountie, anyway?" asked Jeff.

Peter shrugged. "Who else?"

There was the tapping of leather boots. The Mountie appeared, eyes clear, back ramrod straight. Splendid in his scarlet tunic and tan Stetson, Mike Smith marched smartly up to take his mount.

"It figures," Wiley mumbled.

"All right, Iceman," Jeff sighed. "How does this work? We're not a real horse, just in case you haven't noticed."

"Leave everything to me," promised Mike, and Jeff could have sworn that his voice was deeper than before. He pulled the costume over Jeff's head and buttoned it to the back of Wiley's half.

Bent over and smothering, Jeff gasped, "Don't sit on my head!"

But when Mike mounted up, he was perched on Jeff's shoulders.

"Hold it! Time out—" Jeff wheezed.

At that moment they heard Christy's voice over the PA: ". . . those defenders of truth and justice, upholders of the law of the land, *the Royal Canadian Mounted Police*!"

Wiley stepped forward, and Jeff almost overbalanced and fell on his face. Somchow, he managed to stumble along. What the audience saw was a tall handsome Mountie riding toward them.

"A horsey! A horsey!" The kindergartners ceased their candy hunt, and ran to mob the horse. Even the weary crowd came back to life and applauded the spectacle.

"Hey, slow down! Not so fast!" Jeff shuffled at top speed, trying to keep up with Wiley.

"Don't be such a wimp!" Wiley tossed over his shoulder.

"Yeah, I'd like to see you carry around a thousand-pound guy!"

"At least I wouldn't make a big stink about it, like you!"

Enraged, Jeff reached forward, grabbed Wiley by the shoulder, and spun him around. Perched above the costume, Mike Smith lurched with the sudden movement, but steadied himself.

"You lousy creep!" Jeff raged. "I'm not even supposed to *be* here! It's hot, it's dark, it smells, and I'm sweating like Mr. Huge! I can't find my mustache, my back is breaking, and it's all your fault!"

Wiley snorted. "Does Cassandra know what a crybaby you are?"

Taking a shot in the dark, Jeff punched him in the side of the head. Wiley wheeled and jabbed Jeff in the stomach. Jeff grabbed Wiley around the neck, and the two began to wrestle.

Mike Smith lurched forward, and then back. He grabbed the reins and held on, bouncing wildly as the costume wrenched with the violent motions of the fighters below.

Mike's heart was pounding in his throat. What was going on down there? And what could he do *now*? He was in the spotlight in front of hundreds of people!

He was about to panic when a voice called out, "Ride 'em, Iceman!"

He stared. His classmates had assembled in front of the Canada display. They were rooting for him, the way they always did.

"Hang on, Iceman!"

"You can do it!"

Mike felt a surge of emotion. And suddenly he knew that he *could* do it. He would ride this bucking bronco, and make his friends proud.

As Wiley and Jeff fought inside the costume, the intrepid Mountie rode his kicking horse, hanging on to the saddle horn with one hand. With the other, he waved his Stetson to the crowd.

The audience rose to its feet in a tumultuous standing ovation. With the guests rose the teachers and students of OOPS in howling tribute to the star of the show, Mike Smith.

Mr. Hughes and Cassandra were jumping up and down, screaming with exhilaration. Mr. Doncaster applauded madly, yelling, "*Bravo!*"

Nobody could see that none of this was in the script—that the "bucking" was really two longtime friends brawling inside a horse suit. And when Wiley and Jeff finally collapsed from sheer exhaustion, the audience saw only the amazing Canadian Mountie taming his wild steed.

Mike Smith hopped down and tore the costume off Wiley and Jeff. "Take a bow, you guys!"

The three stood in the spotlight, drinking in the roar of the crowd. In all the excitement, no one noticed that the two halves of the horse both had bloody noses.

COCKROACHES ARE SMARTER THAN US

JEFF BARELY SLEPT a wink all night, and it had nothing to do with his cuts and bruises.

Even as babies, he and Wiley had never laid a hand on each other. They had always "played nice," as their mothers put it. Jeff snorted, which made his nose throb with pain. That eleven-year streak had come to an end in a hurricane of flying knuckles last night.

He climbed gingerly out of bed and examined himself in the mirror. Grotesque was the only word for what he saw. Dried blood was caked under his nose, which meant it must have started bleeding again during the night. A black eye and two fat lips completed the grisly picture.

Jeff watched his battered features form into a lopsided smile. Next door, he knew, Wiley looked just as bad, if not worse. In Mr. Huge language, he and Wiley had put a hundred-and-ten percent into pummeling each other. Cassandra had screamed in shock at the sight of them. Of course, she thought their injuries had come from the Mountie's kicking feet, not from World War III.

Mrs. Greenbaum had been a lot harder to convince.

"What Mountie?" she had asked last night while dabbing at his cuts with stinging iodine. "They don't have Mounties in Mexico. They have Los Federales."

"My country got switched."

"By who?" she'd persisted.

"By the rottenest person in the world."

Tenderly, Jeff washed his face. He felt like he didn't even *know* Wiley anymore. His best friend had turned total stranger almost overnight. How could Wiley stab him in the back again and again and again? The guy would stop at nothing to get Cassandra to ask him to the Sadie Hawkins dance. How long would it be before he kidnapped D. D. and took him over to the old Gunhold place without Jeff?

He threw on jeans and a sweatshirt. Calling, "Mom, I'm going to Wiley's," he left the house. His destination: the toolshed. He, not Wiley, would be the one to take D. D. to Cassandra. It was time to double-cross the double-crosser.

As he slid open the metal door, he had a vision of himself and Cassandra on Sadie Hawkins night. Hmmm. He should probably sign up for some dancing lessons. . . .

He stepped inside the shed and froze. The laundry basket wasn't there. *D. D. was gone!*

"Wiley!" he gasped. His best friend had nabbed D. D. first!

Jeff ran like he'd never run before, ignoring the fact that every pounding footfall made his aches and pains explode. He sprinted past OOPS, and through the sprawling subdivisions on the other side of the school. There still might be time to stop Wiley from claiming all the credit for D. D.

He turned the corner onto Farm Lane and froze. There, fifty feet up the dirt road, was Wiley, struggling along with the laundry basket.

Jeff swallowed the impulse to cry out. He crept up behind Wiley and yanked the basket away, holding the screen in place with his elbow.

"What the—" Wiley's eyes bulged, then narrowed.

"I used to have a really good friend," seethed Jeff. "His name was Wiley. He looked a lot like you, only he wasn't *the biggest slimeball sleazebag who ever lived*!"

Guiltily, Wiley studied the ground. All at once, his battered face snapped back up. "Hey, how did you know D. D. was missing?" He reached out a lightning fist, and locked it onto the plastic mesh of the laundry basket. "You were going to take him yourself, weren't you?"

"Let go!" rasped Jeff.

"Make me!" panted Wiley.

D. D. darted around his blanket, warbling his distress as their tug of war twisted and shook his home.

The earsplitting blast of an air horn made them both wheel. A bulldozer was approaching, its raised blade bouncing as it roared along the rutted dirt road.

Both boys jumped back, releasing their grips at the same instant. The screen fell to the ground, but the basket overturned, trapping the sparrow inside. The agitated bird flapped helplessly against the bars of his prison as the bulldozer bore down on him.

"D. D.!!" Wiley and Jeff cried out in agony.

Both covered their eyes as the heavy caterpillar treads squashed the laundry basket flat as a tortilla.

There was a warble of anguish, and then—nothing.

Wiley and Jeff turned accusing fingers on each other. "This is *your* fault!" they chorused.

As the dozer churned past in a cloud of dust, the plastic basket popped back up to its original shape, rolling on the uneven road. A blur of brown and blue shot out of it, flying high above them. D. D. circled in the air, gliding and soaring, free at last. The blue-crested warbler sparrow swooped one last time over the laundry basket and disappeared into the bright autumn sun.

"Way to go," growled Wiley. "Now we've lost our bird."

"I only let go because I thought you were holding on," Jeff defended himself.

"I thought *you* were holding on."

"Wiley? Jeff?" came a distant call.

The two looked around. They were alone except for the tall oaks and weeping willows.

"Up here!" the faint voice insisted.

A glimpse of white woodwork poked out above the tops of the trees at the end of Farm Lane. It was the third floor of the old Gunhold place. At the window stood Cassandra, waving and beckoning. "I'll meet you in the yard!"

The two stood scowling at each other for a long moment.

"Okay, we'll go," Wiley said finally. "But only to ask Cassandra once and for all which one of us she's taking to the dance. After that, I'm never going to say another word to you as long as I live."

"Suits me just fine," Jeff agreed. "Eleven years is eleven too many to be friends with the likes of you."

As they walked along the dirt road, the rest of the Gunhold property came into view. The *Levy* property now, Jeff reminded himself. And what he saw astonished him. A shiny new coat of paint made the Victorian home gleam like a jewel against the surrounding greenery. The shutters and gables had been redone in a soft green, giving the old house a fairy-tale appearance. The crumbling rust was gone from the wrought-iron fence. Instead of knee-high weeds there was a green rolling lawn. Could this be the same place that seemed fit only for the wrecking ball a month ago?

Wiley was thinking the same thing. "Maybe the Levys aren't so stupid after all."

They were perplexed to note that the bulldozer was parked at the corner of the property.

Cassandra exploded down the brand-new front

steps, and came running out to greet them. The folds of her skirt displayed a vast crossword puzzle.

Wiley pointed at the heavy equipment. "You're not knocking the place down after all your hard work?"

She laughed. "They're digging our new swimming pool today." She put an arm around each of them. "Listen, I'm glad you're both here. I have to talk to you about something really important. You know the Sadie Hawkins dance?"

"I think I remember hearing something about it," replied Jeff in a strained voice.

"Well, you guys are my best friends," she said. "So what do you think of this idea—"

Wiley and Jeff exchanged a look that was supercharged with tension. Cassandra had reached her decision.

She blushed. "Do you think I could ask—I mean, would it be a good *idea*—is it even possible—"

This was torture! Jeff could feel a Mr. Huge–size sweat building up on his brow.

"This is *so* hard," Cassandra continued, embarrassed. "How can I put it?"

"Just say it!" they cried in unison.

She blurted it out. "Do you think I should ask the Iceman to the Sadie Hawkins dance?"

"The *Iceman*?!" Wiley repeated in horror.

Jeff felt his blood run cold.

"Oh, sure, I know," Cassandra admitted. "He's the coolest guy in school, and I'm just the new girl—"

"But . . . but . . ." Wiley stammered. "But you don't even *know* Mike Smith."

"Sure I do!" Cassandra exclaimed. "He's up in my room right now!"

"What?" Jeff croaked.

"Well, I didn't get to meet him until last night. After you three put on that amazing show, I went over to congratulate him. Turns out we both like Rollerblading, so I asked him if he wanted to go today, and he said yes." She took a deep breath. "So, what about the dance? Should I invite him or not?"

"Absolutely not," Wiley said, white-lipped.

"Too risky," Jeff mumbled around a paralyzed tongue.

She nodded slowly, pacing in a small circle. "What I need is a sign. Something to tell me I'm doing the right thing."

At that very moment, Mike poked his head and shoulders out of the third-story window. As he waved shyly down at them, a small bird descended from the sky to land on his outstretched arm. Jeff was the first to pick out the bright blue crest. He and Wiley exchanged a look of shock.

It was D. D.!

The normally timid bird hopped up Mike's arm and perched on his shoulder.

Cassandra shrieked in pure joy. "It's—it's—a blue-crested warbler sparrow!" She turned a bright pink face on Wiley and Jeff. "That's my sign!"

"It's only a robin!" Wiley babbled. "Or a starling! Or a really big moth! It's a—"

But Cassandra was already sprinting for the front door, shouting, "Iceman, would you be my date at the Sadie Hawkins dance?"

Her words rattled between Jeff's ears. How many thousands of times had he imagined that question? And what was Mike's answer?

"Well, okay, but I think I let a bird in your house."

It wasn't fair. It wasn't even close to fair. There couldn't be a *millionth* of an ounce of fairness in a world where you could nickname a complete zero, then have him *become* his nickname, and steal away the girl of your dreams. It was too much to bear!

One look at the thundercloud that was Wiley's face, and Jeff knew his friend was thinking the same thing. And in a strange way, the pain felt almost *right.* After eleven years of sharing practically everything, it seemed proper that Wiley Adamson and Jeff Greenbaum should also share their first broken heart.

By unspoken agreement, the two turned their backs on the old Gunhold place and walked out the gate. Neither spoke until they were halfway down Farm Lane.

Suddenly, both boys stopped in their tracks and chorused, "Carrot-top."

Wiley nodded. "Definitely. That's the nickname we've been looking for."

"Why didn't we think of it before?" Jeff mused.

"We did," replied Wiley. "And we junked it. We were idiots."

"D. D. is smarter than us," Jeff agreed.

"Cockroaches are smarter than us," Wiley amended.

"Parasites."

"Plants."

Wiley pointed. "See that rock over there? That guy is a genius compared to us."

He put an arm around Jeff's shoulders, and the two nicknamers walked home without another word.

chapter 17

WORST TO FIRST

THE DIM BULBS of 6B scored in the top one percent on the State Reading Assessment. It was the greatest improvement in the history of the test. Mr. Hughes was signed to a full-time teaching contract at Old Orchard Public School. After all, any teacher who could bring his class from worst to first in a few short weeks was a treasure for his school.

Mr. Hughes never found out that the 6B marathon had saved his job.

"And he never will," Cassandra decided, "as long as we keep on reading. He'll only get suspicious if we stop."

By this time reading had become almost a way of

life in Mr. Hughes's class. Cassandra's plan was going to be a piece of cake.

Of course, no one was calling her Cassandra anymore. Wiley and Jeff worked their magic, and the name Carrot-top caught on like a brush fire. The person who liked it best was Cassandra herself. She even added a new skirt to her famous collection. It was blue denim, with *Carrot-top* spelled out in nail studs.

She'd worn it for the first time on a very special occasion. It was the day that she, Mike Smith, Wiley, and Jeff had released D. D. back into the wild. On the spot, the four had decided to form the Endangered Species Club at school. Wiley and Jeff were already hard at work inventing nicknames for all the endangered animals, starting with the bald eagle—Old Chrome-dome.

The nicknamers had agreed to forgive Cassandra for not believing that they had rescued D. D. first. Wiley said that one day, when they were eighty—maybe—they might even forgive her for taking Mike to the Sadie Hawkins dance.

Secretly, Jeff was grateful to Cassandra for choosing Mike. If she had invited Wiley or Jeff, the odd man out would have been devastated. The bad feelings might have ripped apart their friendship. And while

Cassandra was pretty special, a friend like Wiley came around once in a hundred lifetimes.

There was only one loose end, one thing left undone.

"Snoopy—I mean, *Charles*," said Wiley at recess. "We were wrong and you were right." He took a deep breath. "*Man*, were you ever right!"

"So you don't have to be Snoopy anymore," Jeff went on. "We'll call you whatever you say. We'll even help spread it around so it catches on."

"Don't you dare!" exclaimed Charles. "I've got the best nickname at school—next to the Iceman, of course."

Wiley was astonished. "But you *hate* being Snoopy! That's what this was all about, remember?"

"Hah!" Charles was triumphant. "If it wasn't for my snooping, we never would have found out that Mr. Huge was going to get fired. I saved our teacher. I'm *proud* to be Snoopy!"

They watched him walk off, head high.

"Well, he's happy," Jeff commented.

Wiley looked thoughtful. "You know, there's got to be a better nickname for that guy."

Jeff nodded. "We'll start working on it right away."

When Mr. Hughes was invited to speak at the next school board meeting, the room was packed.

Everyone was anxious to hear the secrets of the star of the State Reading Assessment.

The lecture started off quietly, but soon the big teacher's coaching instincts took over. Three minutes into his speech he was galloping up and down the stage, guzzling Gatorade, sweating and howling. 6B would have been right at home with this performance. But the school board was completely cowed.

"Any questions?" rasped Mr. Hughes after ten very loud minutes.

Shocked silence.

At last, a young teacher in the front row raised her hand. "How would you describe your approach to the reading test?"

"Picture this!" cried Mr. Hughes. "Fourth down! No time-outs! *And we threw the long bomb!*" To illustrate, he reared back and hurled the portable microphone through the picture window and out into the parking lot.

The president of the school board turned frantically to Mr. Doncaster. "Good heavens, man! What is he doing?"

He got the deer-in-headlights look in return. "Isn't it obvious?" the principal replied. "He's giving a hundred-and-ten percent."

WANT MORE GORDON KORMAN?

Turn the page to start reading!

1

NAME: CAPRICORN ANDERSON

I was thirteen the first time I saw a police officer up close. He was arresting me for driving without a license. At the time, I didn't even know what a license was. I wasn't too clear on what being arrested meant either.

But by then they were loading Rain onto a stretcher to rush her in for X-rays. So I barely noticed the handcuffs the officer slapped on my wrists.

"Who's the owner of this pickup?"

"It belongs to the community," I told him.

He made a note on a ring-bound pad. "What community? Golf club? Condo deal?"

"Garland Farm."

He frowned. "Never heard of that one."

Rain would have been pleased. That was the whole point of the community—to allow us to escape the money-hungry rat race of modern society. If people didn't know us, they couldn't find us, and we could live our lives in peace.

"It's an alternative farm commune," I explained.

The officer goggled at me. "Alternative—you mean like *hippies*?"

"Rain used to be one, back in the sixties. There were fourteen families at Garland then. Now it's just Rain and me." I tried to edge my way toward the nursing station. "I have to make sure she's okay."

He was unmoved. "Who is this Rain? According to her Social Security card, the patient's name is Rachel Esther Rosenblatt."

"Her name is Rain, and she's my grandmother," I said stiffly. "She fell out of a tree."

He stared at his notes. "What was a sixty-seven-year-old woman doing up a tree?"

"Picking plums," I replied defensively. "She slipped."

"So you drove her here. At thirteen."

"I drive all the time," I informed him. "Rain taught me when I was eight."

Sweat appeared on his upper lip. "And you never thought of just dialing 911?"

I regarded him blankly. "What's nine-one-one?"

"The emergency number! On the telephone!"

I told him the truth. "I've talked on a telephone a couple of times. In town. But we don't have one."

He looked at me for what seemed like forever. "What's your name, son?"

"Cap. It's short for Capricorn."

He unlocked my handcuffs. I was un-arrested.

How could an able-bodied teenager allow his grandmother to scale a plum tree? Simple. She wasn't my grandmother at the time. She was my teacher.

I was homeschooled. That was the law. Even on a tiny farm like ours, you had to get an education. No school bus could ever make it up the rutted, snaking dirt road that led to Garland. But transportation wasn't the only problem. If we'd been serviced by an eight-lane highway, Rain still would have handled my schooling personally. We wanted to avoid the low standards and cultural poison of a world that had lost its way.

So that's what I was doing when Rain fell—working on a vocabulary lesson. Most of the list came from the state eighth grade curriculum: *barometer*, *decagon*, *perpendicular* . . .

I could always spot the extra words Rain threw in: *non-violence*, *Zen Buddhism*, *psychedelic* . . .

Microprocessor? I frowned at the paper on the unpainted wooden table. Was that Rain or the state? I'd never heard that term before.

I stepped out of the house, careful not to disturb my science project—the Foucault pendulum suspended from the porch roof. The tester from the education department thought it was good enough to enter in the county science fair. Too bad we didn't believe in competition—all that emphasis on trophies and medals, the shiny symbols of an empty soul. Anyway, Rain said the whole thing was a trick to get me to go to regular school.

"If your project is excellent, it only proves that you're getting a superior education right here with me" had been her reasoning.

I spotted her up in the tree, reaching across a limb to pick a plum. "Rain," I called, "there's a word I don't under—"

And it happened. One minute she was on the branch; the next she was on the ground. I don't even recall seeing her fall. Just the faint cry followed by the dull clunk.

"Aaah!" *Whump*.

"Rain!"

She was lying on her side amid the scattered plums when I pounded onto the scene. Her face was very pale. She wasn't moving.

My terror was total. Rain was everything to me—my teacher, my family, my whole universe. Garland was a community, but *we* were the community—the two of us!

I knelt beside her. "Rain—are you okay? Please be okay!"

Her eyes fluttered open and focused on me. She tried to smile, but the pain contorted her expression into a grimace. "Cap—" she began faintly.

I leaped back to my feet. "I'll get Doc Cafferty!"

Doc Cafferty lived a few miles away. He was technically a veterinarian. But he was used to working on humans, since he had six kids. He'd given me stitches once when I was eight.

She reached up a tremulous hand and gripped my arm. "We need a real doctor this time. A people doctor."

I stared at her like she was speaking a foreign language. Doc Cafferty had filled all of Garland's medical needs as long as I could remember.

She spelled it out. "You're going to have to take me to the hospital."

* * *

Rain always said that anger upsets the balance inside a person. So when you yell at somebody, you're attacking yourself more than whoever it is you're yelling at.

Falling out of the tree must have made her forget this. Because when the nurses finally let me in to see her, she was screaming at the doctor at top volume. "*I can't do eight weeks of rehab! I can't do eight days!*"

"You've got no choice," the doctor said matter-of-factly. "You have a broken hip. It has to be pinned. After that you'll need extensive physical therapy. It's a long process, and you can't ignore it just because it doesn't fit in with your plans."

"You're not listening!" Rain shrilled. "I'm the caregiver to my grandson! The only caregiver!"

"What about the parents?" the doctor asked. "Where are they?"

She shook her head. "Long dead. Malaria. They were with the Peace Corps in Namibia. They gave their lives for what they believed in."

That sounds worse than it is. But I never knew my parents except from old pictures. They left when I was little. Besides, the rule at Garland back then was that we all belonged to each other, and it didn't matter who was related by blood. I have a few vague recollections of other people in the community when I was really young. But whether they were my parents or not, I can't tell. Anyway, it's impossible to miss what you never had.

I rushed to my grandmother's bedside. "Are you okay? Is your leg all fixed up?"

She looked grave. "We've got a problem, Cap. And you know what we do with problems."

"We talk it out, think it out, work it out," I said readily. It had been that way since the very beginning of Garland in 1967, long before I was born. Now that there were only two of us, Rain still gave me a full vote. She never treated me like I was just a kid.

The doctor was growing impatient. "How about cousins? Or maybe a close friend from school?"

"I'm homeschooled," I supplied.

The doctor sighed. "Mrs. Rosenblatt—"

"That name hasn't applied to me for decades. You can call me Rain."

"All right. Rain. I'm admitting you now. We'll operate in the morning. And I'll call social services to see what arrangements can be made for your grandson."

That was when I started to worry about what was going to happen to me.